British Library Women Writers

STORIES FOR WINTER

AND NIGHTS BY THE FIRE

This anthology first published in 2023 by
The British Library
96 Euston Road
London NW1 2DB

Cataloguing in Publication Data
A catalogue record for this publication is available from the British Library

ISBN 978 0 7123 5469 1
e-ISBN 978 0 7123 6876 6

Series editor Alison Moss
Series consultant Simon Thomas

Text design and typesetting by JCS Publishing Services Ltd
Printed and bound by CPI Group (UK), Croydon, CR0 4YY

CONTENTS

INTRODUCTION

What do you expect to find in a collection of short stories set during winter? Christmas short stories often dominate the season, and the Women Writers anthology *Stories for Christmas and the Festive Season* collected a wide variety of stories covering the usual and unusual experiences of women through the decades and generations over those special, hectic, often poignant days.

But winter is, of course, much more than Christmas. In *Stories for Winter and Nights by the Fire*, you'll discover many and varied tales from the short days and long nights of winter. These stories focus on the particular experiences of women throughout the twentieth century – reflecting the changing roles and rights of women over this period, and the way that their public and private lives were influenced by this flux. You'll find women judged by their appearance, experiencing unequal power dynamics in marriage, battling against restrictions and exploring new freedoms – as well as rejoicing in sisterly relationships.

In the following pages, the stories are arranged in the chronological order they were published – but perhaps you won't want to read the stories in the order they're laid out. Perhaps

you'll dart between well-known names such as Edith Wharton, Katherine Mansfield and Angela Carter to lesser-known authors such as Elizabeth Banks, Frances Bellerby and Kate Roberts. It's fun to explore the unexpected links between stories written in different countries, decades and styles. And that's what this introduction will do, looking for some of those surprising points of connection, as well as providing a little background to each of the authors.

To return to that first question: what do you expect in a wintery story? In the northern hemisphere, at least, the answer is probably snow. And none of the stories in this collection are snowier than 'The Snowstorm' (1935) by Violet M. MacDonald, which, unseasonably, first appeared in a June edition of *Lovat Dickson's Magazine*.

> Sifting down past the window she saw a fine, dense, veil of snow. The whole world had turned a pale, ashen colour: furry blocks of wall and roof and chimney outlined dimly on a pinkish sky.

Elizabeth and her unnamed companion drive along 'a white tunnel progressively bored out of blackness', and 'the world seemed dissolving under the gentle, insistent action of the snow'. Both literal and metaphorical worlds seem to be dissolving, and this enclosing winter is the perfect setting for a fleeting romance. Little is known about MacDonald, except that she worked as a writer and translator from French, German and Russian.

⁂ ⁂ ⁂

A car and the aftermath of love are central in 'A Motor' (1922) by Elizabeth Bibesco, in which two strangers unwittingly find unity in encountering a particular motor car, reflecting on past romances and separately enjoying a 'special quality about a December sunset'. It's one of the shortest stories in the collection: Bibesco was commended by a contemporary reviewer for her 'genius for compression – the compression into a few phrases of all the details of a situation, into a few pages of the hopes and failures of a lifetime'. Better known during her lifetime as a socialite, Bibesco was the daughter of Prime Minister Herbert Asquith.

Although only written twenty years earlier, Edith Wharton's 'The Reckoning' (1902) may feel like it's from another era in its controversies about a 'modern marriage'. Julia and Clement Westall are facing a dilemma in the terms they had agreed that a marriage must be founded on 'a solemn agreement between the contracting parties to keep faith with themselves, and not to live together for a moment after complete accord had ceased to exist between them'. A short winter's day is the backdrop to the true testing of this resolve, with the darkness of New York's streets used to good effect in Julia's moment of crisis. One of the most revered American writers of her period, Edith Wharton remains famed for novels including *The Age of Innocence* and *The House of Mirth*, and in 1921 was the first woman to win the Pulitzer Prize for fiction.

Winter seems the period for uncertain relationships. Rose and Gilbert are the couple at the heart of 'The Thames Spread

⁂ ⁂ ⁂

Out' (1959) by Elizabeth Taylor. In the story, Rose will have an unusual and exhilarating adventure – against the unusual winter backdrop of a river that has burst its banks:

> The sun was beginning to set and she knew how soon it got dark these winter days. She took her cup of tea and went out on to the balcony to watch. Every ten years or so, the Thames in that place would rise too high, brim over its banks and cover the fields for miles, changing the landscape utterly.

Taylor is often mentioned in lists of the 'most underrated authors', and sometimes as 'the other Elizabeth Taylor' so as not to confuse her with the actress. Her novels have all been discovered and reprinted, and she is increasingly revered for works including *Mrs Palfrey at the Claremont* and *Angel*.

Following the river to the sea, we find two very different stories that take place at the seaside. More often the location for summery stories, both Frances Bellerby and Angela Carter take us to the coast for winter. In Bellerby's 'The Cut Finger' (1948) 5-year-old Julia has a moment of horrifying realisation during a stay by the sea. In Carter's 'The Smile of Winter' (1974), meanwhile, pacing the shore and collecting shells is an opportunity for the author's characteristically poetic, searing prose:

> From morning until evening, a hallucinatory light floods the shore and a cool, glittering sun transfigures everything so

brilliantly that the beach looks like a desert and the ocean like a mirage.

During her lifetime, Bellerby was chiefly considered as a poet, with 'Voices' her most-remembered work. Carter is likely to be more familiar to most readers. Her novels include *Nights at the Circus*, *Wise Children* and *The Magic Toyshop*, and she has had generations of fans, both for her magical realism and for her influential incorporation of feminism into her novels and short stories.

For many British people, the first thing to think of to accompany a winter night by the fire is a cup of tea – and a cup of tea is pivotal in two of the stories in this collection. It brings together people from two very different situations in Elizabeth Berridge's 'The Prisoner' (1947), which opens: 'It was a frosty morning when the German prisoners first came to dig drainage ditches in the fields that lay beyond Miss Everton's garden walls.' Over the course of the story, and over a series of cups of tea, Miss Everton grows to know and connect with Erich, one of the prisoners-of-war. In Berridge's long writing career she published short stories, children's books and novels – including the British Library Women Writers title *Sing Me Who You Are* (1967).

A less successful connection is formed in New Zealand author Katherine Mansfield's 'A Cup of Tea' (1922), in which a wealthy young Rosemary is asked for 'the price of a cup of tea' by a beggar called Miss Smith. Instead, Rosemary takes her home in an act, as Mansfield makes clear, which is less about benevolence on a cold winter's day and more about her own self-indulgence:

> And suddenly it seemed to Rosemary such an adventure. It was like something out of a novel by Dostoevsky, this meeting in the dusk. Supposing she took the girl home? Supposing she did do one of those things she was always reading about or seeing on the stage, what would happen? It would be thrilling.

Jealousy overcomes class in the denouement of this story. 'A Cup of Tea' appeared in *The Doves' Nest and Other Stories* in 1923, the first collection published after Mansfield's death. She was only 34 when she died from tuberculosis and she continues to be regarded as one of the finest writers of the short story.

Poverty hides in plain sight in 'The Woman Who Was So Tired' (1906) by America author Elizabeth Banks. The heroine is working as a 'Little Reporter' and is sent out by her boss on a winter's day with a melancholy brief:

> "New York must be full of suffering of one kind and another on a day like this. Just go out and spend it looking for the coldest woman in New York, or the saddest woman, or the most overworked woman, or the most anything woman in New York, and come back and write a story about her."

Her story about an overworked woman in a poor family leads to the paper being inundated with gifts from the public; but is her boss right in thinking that she's made the woman up? The story initially appeared under the name Mary Mortimer Maxwell, Banks' pseudonym. While living in London, she caused

something of a sensation by posing variously as a housemaid, a street sweeper and a flower girl and using the research to reveal the life of people living in poverty.

Still in New York, but a different echelon, Shirley Jackson's 'My Life with R. H. Macy' (1941) takes us behind the scenes of Macy's department store – a place where Jackson worked as a shop clerk for a period. It was one of the first stories she published, in a Christmas edition of *The New Republic*, and the anonymous drudgery of the protagonist is made clear by her being called only '13-3138'. Eight years later, Jackson would write her most famous and controversial story, 'The Lottery', and is also remembered for gothic-inspired novels including *The Haunting of Hill House* and *We Have Always Lived in the Castle* as well as comic memoirs of family life.

From a department store we move to a much smaller and more mysterious shop, the titular hat shop in 'Ann Lee's' (1926) by Elizabeth Bowen. Miss Ames and Mrs Logan – 'young women with faces of similar pinkness; they used the same swear-words and knew the same men' – are customers at a hat shop which is expensive and peculiar, but provides the perfect headwear for each woman. During their exploration of the many hats, a man intrudes into this female space, bringing a slightly seamy undertone to this everyday shopping experience. Meanwhile, the pursuit of a hat is less satisfactory in Kate Robert's 'Ffair Gaeaf'/'November Fair' (1937), translated from Welsh by Joseph P. Clancy – just one of the episodes marking this event in a small Welsh town:

> "That one suits you splendidly, Mrs. Jones," the shop girl said about every hat that Elin tried on, with Lydia on the other side making faces and shaking her head to show that she didn't agree.

Elizabeth Bowen is a renowned Irish-British novelist whose novels include *The Heat of the Day*, *The Last September* and *The House in Paris*. She was awarded a CBE for literature, and often set her fiction in the sizable houses of Irish Protestant families – though she is also noted for her depictions of wartime London and her ghost stories. Kate Roberts, like Elizabeth Bowen, was born in the 1890s, but while Bowen was born into an Irish gentry family, Roberts was the daughter of a Welsh quarryman. She wrote widely in Welsh and has been styled *Brenhines ein Llên* ('The Queen of our Literature').

However well you've prepared for the winter, and whatever you're planning to do, there is one thing that is guaranteed to knock you off course: the annual cold. Sylvia Townsend Warner takes this predictable ailment – 'What are colds? Everyone has them, they are part of English life' – as the theme of 'The Cold' (1945). Throughout the story, 'Cold' keeps its capital 'C', making it feel like an official visitor heralding an outsize power and significance.

> The Cold came into the household by Mrs. Ryder. At first she said she had picked it up at the Mothers' Union meeting; later—it was the kind of cold that gets worse with time—she

> attributed it to getting chilled through waiting in the village shop while that horrible Beryl Legg took over half an hour to decide whether she would spend her points on salmon or Spam. Never a thought for her child, of course, who by now should be getting prunes and cereals. Whoever the father might be, one would have expected the girl to show some maternal feeling—but no!

As the quote hints, Warner uses the simple cold as a way of exploring underlying class, tensions and prejudices. And while everyone in the household is equally susceptible to the cold, not everyone has the same luxury in recuperating. With her trademark ironic humour, Warner's simple premise tells us more than expected about the life of a working-class woman in the mid-twentieth century.

Sylvia Townsend Warner remains best remembered for her first novel, *Lolly Willowes*, about an unmarried, middle-aged woman who takes a drastic step to guarantee her independence. Although *Lolly Willowes* takes place in the 1920s English countryside, later novels cover such disparate settings as the French Revolution, a medieval nunnery and a missionary trip to the South Sea Islands. Her short stories were mostly published in *The New Yorker*, and for many years were more familiar to an American audience than in her native Britain.

Finally, no book of stories for winter would be complete without a ghost story by Dickens – although, in the case of this collection, you'll find it from the pen of Mary Angela Dickens,

whose 'My Fellow Travellers' (1906) recounts the events of a bitterly cold train journey. The author's surname is no coincidence: Mary Angela Dickens was the eldest grandchild of Charles Dickens, and some of her earliest work appeared in the periodical he founded, *All the Year Round*. As well as novels and short stories, Mary Angela Dickens wrote several children's versions of her grandfather's novels.

Through all the different directions, worlds and characters that these wintery tales take you, hopefully they can accompany an evening by the fire, a mug of something hot and a plate of something festively tasty. There are many familiar authors to meet again and unfamiliar authors to encounter afresh. Happy winter reading!

Simon Thomas

Series consultant **Simon Thomas** created the middlebrow blog Stuck in a Book in 2007. He is also the co-host of the popular podcast Tea or Books? Simon has a PhD from Oxford University in Interwar Literature.

PUBLISHER'S NOTE

These stories, like the original novels reprinted in the British Library Women Writers series, were written and published, for the most part, from the 1910s to the 1950s. There are many elements of these stories which continue to entertain modern readers, however, in some cases there are also uses of language, instances of stereotyping and some attitudes expressed by narrators or characters which may not be endorsed by the publishing standards of today, and we acknowledge may continue to make uncomfortable reading for some of our audience. With this series, British Library Publishing aims to offer a new readership a chance to read some of the rare books of the British Library's collections in an affordable paperback format, to enjoy their merits and to look back into the world of the twentieth century as portrayed by their writers. It is not possible to separate these stories from the history of their writing and as such the stories are presented as originally published with minor edits made for consistency of style and sense. We welcome feedback from our readers, which can be sent to the following address: British Library Publishing, The British Library, 96 Euston Road, London, NW1 2DB.

THE RECKONING

Edith Wharton

I

"The marriage law of the new dispensation will be: *Thou shalt not be unfaithful—to thyself.*"

A discreet murmur of approval filled the studio, and through the haze of cigarette smoke Mrs. Clement Westall, as her husband descended from his improvised platform, saw him merged in a congratulatory group of ladies. Westall's informal talks on "The New Ethics" had drawn about him an eager following of the mentally unemployed—those who, as he had once phrased it, liked to have their brain-food cut up for them. The talks had begun by accident. Westall's ideas were known to be "advanced," but hitherto their advance had not been in the direction of publicity. He had been, in his wife's opinion, almost pusillanimously careful not to let his personal views endanger his professional standing. Of late, however, he had shown a puzzling tendency to dogmatize, to throw down the gauntlet, to flaunt his private code in the face of society; and the relation of the sexes being a topic always sure of an audience, a few admiring friends had persuaded him to give his after-dinner opinions a larger circulation by summing them up in a series of talks at the Van Sideren studio.

The Herbert Van Siderens were a couple who subsisted, socially, on the fact that they had a studio. Van Sideren's pictures were chiefly valuable as accessories to the *mise en scène* which differentiated his wife's "afternoons" from the blighting functions held in long New York drawing-rooms, and permitted her to offer their friends whiskey-and-soda instead of tea. Mrs. Van Sideren, for her part, was skilled in making the most of the kind of atmosphere which a lay-figure and an easel create; and if at times she found the illusion hard to maintain, and lost courage to the extent of almost wishing that Herbert could paint, she promptly overcame such moments of weakness by calling in some fresh talent, some extraneous re-enforcement of the "artistic" impression. It was in quest of such aid that she had seized on Westall, coaxing him, somewhat to his wife's surprise, into a flattered participation in her fraud. It was vaguely felt, in the Van Sideren circle, that all the audacities were artistic, and that a teacher who pronounced marriage immoral was somehow as distinguished as a painter who depicted purple grass and a green sky. The Van Sideren set were tired of the conventional color-scheme in art and conduct.

Julia Westall had long had her own views on the immorality of marriage; she might indeed have claimed her husband as a disciple. In the early days of their union she had secretly resented his disinclination to proclaim himself a follower of the new creed; had been inclined to tax him with moral cowardice, with a failure to live up to the convictions for which their marriage was supposed to stand. That was in the first burst of propagandism, when, womanlike, she wanted to turn her disobedience into a law. Now she felt differently. She could hardly account for the change, yet being a woman who never allowed her impulses to remain unaccounted for, she tried to do so by saying that she did not care to have the articles of her faith misinterpreted by the vulgar. In this connection, she was beginning to think that almost every one was vulgar; certainly there were few to whom she would have cared to intrust the defence of so esoteric a doctrine. And it was precisely at this point that Westall, discarding his unspoken principles, had chosen to descend from the heights of privacy, and stand hawking his convictions at the street-corner!

It was Una Van Sideren who, on this occasion, unconsciously focussed upon herself Mrs. Westall's wandering resentment. In the first place, the girl had no business to be there. It was "horrid"—Mrs. Westall found herself slipping back into the old feminine vocabulary—simply "horrid" to think of a young girl's being allowed to listen to such talk. The fact that Una smoked cigarettes and sipped an occasional cocktail did not in the least tarnish a certain radiant innocency which made her appear the victim, rather than the accomplice, of her parents' vulgarities. Julia Westall felt in a hot helpless way that something ought to be done—that some one ought to speak to the girl's mother. And just then Una glided up.

"Oh, Mrs. Westall, how beautiful it was!" Una fixed her with large limpid eyes. "You believe it all, I suppose?" she asked with seraphic gravity.

"All—what, my dear child?"

The girl shone on her. "About the higher life—the freer expansion of the individual—the law of fidelity to one's self," she glibly recited.

Mrs. Westall, to her own wonder, blushed a deep and burning blush.

"My dear Una," she said, "you don't in the least understand what it's all about!"

Miss Van Sideren stared, with a slowly answering blush. "Don't *you*, then?" she murmured.

Mrs. Westall laughed. "Not always—or altogether! But I should like some tea, please."

Una led her to the corner where innocent beverages were dispensed. As Julia received her cup she scrutinized the girl more carefully. It was not such a girlish face, after all—definite lines were forming under the rosy haze of youth. She reflected that Una must be six-and-twenty, and wondered why she had not married. A nice stock of ideas she would have as her dower! If *they* were to be a part of the modern girl's trousseau—

Mrs. Westall caught herself up with a start. It was as though some one else had been speaking—a stranger who had borrowed her own voice: she felt herself the dupe of some fantastic mental ventriloquism. Concluding suddenly that the room was stifling and Una's tea too sweet, she set down her cup, and looked about for Westall: to meet his eyes had long been her refuge from every uncertainty. She met them now, but only, as she felt, in transit; they included her parenthetically in a larger flight. She followed the flight, and it carried her to a corner to which Una had withdrawn—one of the palmy nooks to which Mrs. Van Sideren attributed the success of her Saturdays. Westall, a moment later, had overtaken his look, and found a place at the girl's side. She bent forward, speaking eagerly; he leaned back, listening, with the depreciatory smile which acted as a filter to flattery, enabling him to swallow the strongest doses without apparent grossness of appetite. Julia winced at her own definition of the smile.

On the way home, in the deserted winter dusk, Westall surprised his wife by a sudden boyish pressure of her arm. "Did I open their eyes a bit? Did I tell them what you wanted me to?" he asked gaily.

Almost unconsciously, she let her arm slip from his. "What *I* wanted—?"

"Why, haven't you—all this time?" She caught the honest wonder of his tone. "I somehow fancied you'd rather blamed me for not talking more openly—before—You've made me feel, at times, that I was sacrificing principles to expediency."

She paused a moment over her reply; then she asked quietly: "What made you decide not to—any longer?"

She felt again the vibration of a faint surprise. "Why—the wish to please you!" he answered, almost too simply.

"I wish you would not go on, then," she said abruptly.

He stopped in his quick walk, and she felt his stare through the darkness.

"Not go on—?"

"Call a hansom, please. I'm tired," broke from her with a sudden rush of physical weariness.

Instantly his solicitude enveloped her. The room had been infernally hot—and then that confounded cigarette smoke—he had noticed once or twice that she looked pale—she mustn't come to another Saturday. She felt herself yielding, as she always did, to the warm influence of his concern for her, the feminine in her leaning on the man in him with a conscious intensity of abandonment. He put her in the hansom, and her hand stole into his in the darkness.

A tear or two rose, and she let them fall. It was so delicious to cry over imaginary troubles!

That evening, after dinner, he surprised her by reverting to the subject of his talk. He combined a man's dislike of uncomfortable questions with an almost feminine skill in eluding them; and she knew that if he returned to the subject he must have some special reason for doing so.

"You seem not to have cared for what I said this afternoon. Did I put the case badly?"

"No—you put it very well."

"Then what did you mean by saying that you would rather not have me go on with it?"

She glanced at him nervously, her ignorance of his intention deepening her sense of helplessness.

"I don't think I care to hear such things discussed in public."

"I don't understand you," he exclaimed. Again the feeling that his surprise was genuine gave an air of obliquity to her own attitude. She was not sure that she understood herself.

"Won't you explain?" he said with a tinge of impatience.

Her eyes wandered about the familiar drawing-room which had been the scene of so many of their evening confidences. The shaded lamps, the quiet-colored walls hung with mezzotints, the pale spring flowers scattered here and there in Venice glasses and bowls of old Sevres, recalled, she hardly knew why, the apartment in which the evenings of her first marriage had been passed—a wilderness of rosewood and upholstery, with a picture of a Roman peasant above the mantel-piece, and a Greek slave in "statuary marble" between the folding-doors of the back drawing-room. It was a room with which she had never been able to establish any closer relation than that between a traveller and a railway station; and now, as she looked about at the surroundings which stood for her deepest affinities—the room for which she had left that other room—she was startled by the same sense of strangeness and unfamiliarity. The prints, the flowers, the subdued tones of the old porcelains, seemed to typify a superficial refinement that had no relation to the deeper significances of life.

Suddenly she heard her husband repeating his question.

"I don't know that I can explain," she faltered.

He drew his arm-chair forward so that he faced her across the hearth. The light of a reading-lamp fell on his finely drawn face, which had a kind of surface-sensitiveness akin to the surface-refinement of its setting.

"Is it that you no longer believe in our ideas?" he asked.

"In our ideas—?"

"The ideas I am trying to teach. The ideas you and I are supposed to stand for." He paused a moment. "The ideas on which our marriage was founded."

The blood rushed to her face. He had his reasons, then—she was sure now that he had his reasons! In the ten years of their marriage, how often had either of them stopped to consider the ideas on which it was founded? How often does a man dig about the basement of his house to examine its foundation? The foundation is there, of course—the house rests on it—but one lives abovestairs and not in the cellar. It was she, indeed, who in the beginning had insisted on reviewing the situation now and then, on recapitulating the reasons which justified her course, on proclaiming, from time to time, her adherence to the religion of personal independence; but she had long ceased to feel the need of any such ideal standards, and had accepted her marriage as frankly and naturally as though it had been based on the primitive needs of the heart, and needed no special sanction to explain or justify it.

"Of course I still believe in our ideas!" she exclaimed.

"Then I repeat that I don't understand. It was a part of your theory that the greatest possible publicity should be given to our view of marriage. Have you changed your mind in that respect?"

She hesitated. "It depends on circumstances—on the public one is addressing. The set of people that the Van Siderens get about them don't care for the truth or falseness of a doctrine. They are attracted simply by its novelty."

"And yet it was in just such a set of people that you and I met, and learned the truth from each other."

"That was different."

"I thought you considered it one of the deepest social wrongs that such things never *are* discussed before young girls; but that is beside the point, for I don't remember seeing any young girl in my audience to-day—"

"Except Una Van Sideren!"

He turned slightly and pushed back the lamp at his elbow.

"Oh, Miss Van Sideren—naturally—"

"Why naturally?"

"The daughter of the house—would you have had her sent out with her governess?"

"If I had a daughter I should not allow such things to go on in my house!"

Westall, stroking his mustache, leaned back with a faint smile. "I fancy Miss Van Sideren is quite capable of taking care of herself."

"No girl knows how to take care of herself—till it's too late."

"And yet you would deliberately deny her the surest means of self-defence?"

"What do you call the surest means of self-defence?"

"Some preliminary knowledge of human nature in its relation to the marriage tie."

She made an impatient gesture. "How should you like to marry that kind of a girl?"

"Immensely—if she were my kind of girl in other respects."

She took up the argument at another point.

"You are quite mistaken if you think such talk does not affect young girls. Una was in a state of the most absurd exaltation—" She broke off, wondering why she had spoken.

Westall reopened a magazine which he had laid aside at the beginning of their discussion. "What you tell me is immensely flattering to my oratorical talent—but I fear you overrate its effect. I can assure you that Miss Van Sideren doesn't have to have her thinking done for her. She's quite capable of doing it herself."

"You seem very familiar with her mental processes!" flashed unguardedly from his wife.

He looked up quietly from the pages he was cutting.

"I should like to be," he answered. "She interests me."

II

If there be a distinction in being misunderstood, it was one denied to Julia Westall when she left her first husband. Every one was ready to excuse and even to defend her. The world she adorned agreed that John Arment was "impossible," and hostesses gave a sigh of relief at the thought that it would no longer be necessary to ask him to dine.

There had been no scandal connected with the divorce: neither side had accused the other of the offence euphemistically described as "statutory." The Arments had indeed been obliged to transfer their allegiance to a State which recognized desertion as a cause for divorce, and construed the term so liberally that the seeds of desertion were shown to exist in every union. Even Mrs. Arment's second marriage did not make traditional morality stir in its sleep. It was known that she had not met her second husband till after she had parted from the first, and she had, moreover, replaced a rich man by a poor one. Though Clement Westall was acknowledged to be a rising lawyer, it was generally felt that his fortunes would not rise as rapidly as his reputation. The Westalls would probably always have to live quietly and go out to dinner in cabs. Could there be better evidence of Mrs. Arment's complete disinterestedness?

If the reasoning by which her friends justified her course was somewhat cruder and less complex than her own elucidation of the matter, both explanations led to the same conclusion: John Arment was impossible. The only difference was that, to his wife, his impossibility was something deeper than a social disqualification. She had once said, in ironical defence of her marriage, that it had at least preserved her from the necessity of sitting next to him at dinner; but she had not then realized at what cost the immunity was purchased. John Arment was impossible; but the sting of his impossibility lay in the fact that he made it impossible for those about him to be other than himself. By an unconscious process of elimination he had excluded from the world everything of which he did not feel a personal need: had become, as it were, a climate in which only his own requirements survived. This might seem to imply a deliberate selfishness; but there was nothing deliberate about Arment. He was as instinctive as an animal or a child. It was this childish element in his nature which sometimes for a moment unsettled his wife's estimate of him. Was it possible that he was simply undeveloped, that he had delayed, somewhat longer than is usual, the laborious process of growing up? He had the kind of sporadic shrewdness which causes it to be said of a dull man that he is "no fool"; and it was this quality that his wife found most trying. Even to the naturalist it is annoying to have his deductions disturbed by some unforeseen aberrancy of form or function; and how much more so to the wife whose estimate of herself is inevitably bound up with her judgment of her husband!

Arment's shrewdness did not, indeed, imply any latent intellectual power; it suggested, rather, potentialities of feeling, of suffering, perhaps, in a blind rudimentary way, on which Julia's sensibilities naturally declined to linger. She so fully understood her own reasons for leaving him that she disliked to think they were not as comprehensible to her husband. She was haunted, in her analytic moments, by the look of perplexity, too inarticulate for words, with which he had acquiesced to her explanations.

These moments were rare with her, however. Her marriage had been too concrete a misery to be surveyed philosophically. If she had been unhappy for complex reasons, the unhappiness was as real as though it had been uncomplicated. Soul is more bruisable than flesh, and Julia was wounded in every fibre of her spirit. Her husband's personality seemed to be closing gradually in on her, obscuring the sky and cutting off the air, till she felt herself shut up among the decaying bodies of her starved hopes. A sense of having been decoyed by some world-old conspiracy into this bondage of body and soul filled her with despair. If marriage was the slow life-long acquittal of a debt contracted in ignorance, then marriage was a crime against human nature. She, for one, would have no share in maintaining the pretence of which she had been a victim: the pretence that a man and a woman, forced into the narrowest of personal relations, must remain there till the end, though they may have outgrown the span of each other's natures as the mature tree outgrows the iron brace about the sapling.

It was in the first heat of her moral indignation that she had met Clement Westall. She had seen at once that he was "interested," and had fought off the discovery, dreading any influence that should draw her back into the bondage of conventional relations. To ward off the peril she had, with an almost crude precipitancy, revealed her opinions to him. To her surprise, she found that he shared them. She was attracted by the frankness of a suitor who, while pressing his suit, admitted that he did not believe in marriage. Her worst audacities did not seem to surprise him: he had thought out all that she had felt, and they had reached the same conclusion. People grew at varying rates, and the yoke that was an easy fit for the one might soon become galling to the other. That was what divorce was for: the readjustment of personal relations. As soon as their necessarily transitive nature was recognized they would gain in dignity as well as in harmony. There would be no farther need of the ignoble concessions and connivances, the perpetual sacrifice of personal delicacy and moral pride, by means of which imperfect marriages were now held together. Each partner to the contract would be on his mettle, forced to live up to the highest standard of self-development, on pain of losing the other's respect and affection. The low nature could no longer drag the higher down, but must struggle to rise, or remain alone on its inferior level. The only necessary condition to a harmonious marriage was a frank recognition of this truth, and a solemn agreement between the contracting parties to keep faith with themselves, and not to live together for a moment after complete accord had ceased to exist between them. The new adultery was unfaithfulness to self.

It was, as Westall had just reminded her, on this understanding that they had married. The ceremony was an unimportant concession to social prejudice: now that the door of divorce stood open, no marriage need be an imprisonment, and the contract therefore no longer involved any diminution of self-respect. The nature of their attachment placed them so far beyond the reach of such contingencies that it was easy to discuss them with an open mind; and Julia's sense of security made her dwell with a tender insistence on Westall's promise to claim his release when he should cease to love her. The exchange of these vows seemed to make them, in a sense, champions of the new law, pioneers in the forbidden realm of individual freedom: they felt that they had somehow achieved beatitude without martyrdom.

This, as Julia now reviewed the past, she perceived to have been her theoretical attitude toward marriage. It was unconsciously, insidiously, that her ten years of happiness with Westall had developed another conception of the tie; a reversion, rather, to the old instinct of passionate dependency and possessorship that now made her blood revolt at the mere hint of change. Change? Renewal? Was that what they had called it, in their foolish jargon? Destruction, extermination rather—this rending of a myriad fibres interwoven with another's being! Another? But he was not other!

He and she were one, one in the mystic sense which alone gave marriage its significance. The new law was not for them, but for the disunited creatures forced into a mockery of union. The gospel she had felt called on to proclaim had no bearing on her own case. … She sent for the doctor and told him she was sure she needed a nerve tonic.

She took the nerve tonic diligently, but it failed to act as a sedative to her fears. She did not know what she feared; but that made her anxiety the more pervasive. Her husband had not reverted to the subject of his Saturday talks. He was unusually kind and considerate, with a softening of his quick manner, a touch of shyness in his consideration, that sickened her with new fears. She told herself that it was because she looked badly—because he knew about the doctor and the nerve tonic—that he showed this deference to her wishes, this eagerness to screen her from moral draughts; but the explanation simply cleared the way for fresh inferences.

The week passed slowly, vacantly, like a prolonged Sunday. On Saturday the morning post brought a note from Mrs. Van Sideren. Would dear Julia ask Mr. Westall to come half an hour earlier than usual, as there was to be some music after his "talk"? Westall was just leaving for his office when his wife read the note. She opened the drawing-room door and called him back to deliver the message.

He glanced at the note and tossed it aside. "What a bore! I shall have to cut my game of racquets. Well, I suppose it can't be helped. Will you write and say it's all right?"

Julia hesitated a moment, her hand stiffening on the chair-back against which she leaned.

"You mean to go on with these talks?" she asked.

"I—why not?" he returned; and this time it struck her that his surprise was not quite unfeigned. The discovery helped her to find words.

"You said you had started them with the idea of pleasing me—"

"Well?"

"I told you last week that they didn't please me."

"Last week? Oh—" He seemed to make an effort of memory. "I thought you were nervous then; you sent for the doctor the next day."

"It was not the doctor I needed; it was your assurance—"

"My assurance?"

Suddenly she felt the floor fail under her. She sank into the chair with a choking throat, her words, her reasons slipping away from her like straws down a whirling flood.

"Clement," she cried, "isn't it enough for you to know that I hate it?"

He turned to close the door behind them; then he walked toward her and sat down. "What is it that you hate?" he asked gently.

She had made a desperate effort to rally her routed argument.

"I can't bear to have you speak as if—as if—our marriage—were like the other kind—the wrong kind. When I heard you there, the other afternoon, before all those inquisitive gossiping people, proclaiming that husbands and wives had a right to leave each other whenever they were tired—or had seen some one else—"

Westall sat motionless, his eyes fixed on a pattern of the carpet.

"You *have* ceased to take this view, then?" he said as she broke off. "You no longer believe that husbands and wives *are* justified in separating—under such conditions?"

"Under such conditions?" she stammered. "Yes—I still believe that—but how can we judge for others? What can we know of the circumstances—?"

He interrupted her. "I thought it was a fundamental article of our creed that the special circumstances produced by marriage were not to interfere with the full assertion of individual liberty." He paused a moment. "I thought that was your reason for leaving Arment."

She flushed to the forehead. It was not like him to give a personal turn to the argument.

"It was my reason," she said simply.

"Well, then—why do you refuse to recognize its validity now?"

"I don't—I don't—I only say that one can't judge for others."

He made an impatient movement. "This is mere hair-splitting. What you mean is that, the doctrine having served your purpose when you needed it, you now repudiate it."

"Well," she exclaimed, flushing again, "what if I do? What does it matter to us?"

Westall rose from his chair. He was excessively pale, and stood before his wife with something of the formality of a stranger.

"It matters to me," he said in a low voice, "because I do *not* repudiate it."

"Well—?"

"And because I had intended to invoke it as"—

He paused and drew his breath deeply. She sat silent, almost deafened by her heart-beats.—"as a complete justification of the course I am about to take."

Julia remained motionless. "What course is that?" she asked.

He cleared his throat. "I mean to claim the fulfilment of your promise."

For an instant the room wavered and darkened; then she recovered a torturing acuteness of vision. Every detail of her surroundings pressed upon her: the tick of the clock, the slant of sunlight on the wall, the hardness of the chair-arms that she grasped, were a separate wound to each sense.

"My promise—" she faltered.

"Your part of our mutual agreement to set each other free if one or the other should wish to be released."

She was silent again. He waited a moment, shifting his position nervously; then he said, with a touch of irritability: "You acknowledge the agreement?"

The question went through her like a shock. She lifted her head to it proudly. "I acknowledge the agreement," she said.

"And—you don't mean to repudiate it?"

A log on the hearth fell forward, and mechanically he advanced and pushed it back.

"No," she answered slowly, "I don't mean to repudiate it."

There was a pause. He remained near the hearth, his elbow resting on the mantel-shelf. Close to his hand stood a little cup of jade that he had given her on one of their wedding anniversaries. She wondered vaguely if he noticed it.

"You intend to leave me, then?" she said at length.

His gesture seemed to deprecate the crudeness of the allusion.

"To marry some one else?"

Again his eye and hand protested. She rose and stood before him.

"Why should you be afraid to tell me? Is it Una Van Sideren?"

He was silent.

"I wish you good luck," she said.

III

She looked up, finding herself alone. She did not remember when or how he had left the room, or how long afterward she had sat there. The fire still smouldered on the hearth, but the slant of sunlight had left the wall.

Her first conscious thought was that she had not broken her word, that she had fulfilled the very letter of their bargain. There had been no crying out, no vain appeal to the past, no attempt at temporizing or evasion. She had marched straight up to the guns.

Now that it was over, she sickened to find herself alive. She looked about her, trying to recover her hold on reality. Her identity seemed to be slipping from her, as it disappears in a physical swoon. "This is my room—this is my house," she heard herself saying. Her room? Her house? She could almost hear the walls laugh back at her.

She stood up, a dull ache in every bone. The silence of the room frightened her. She remembered, now, having heard the front door close a long time ago: the sound suddenly re-echoed through her brain. Her husband must have left the house, then—her *husband?* She no longer knew in what terms to think: the simplest phrases had a poisoned edge. She sank back into her chair, overcome by a strange weakness. The clock struck ten—it was only ten o'clock! Suddenly she remembered that she had not ordered dinner … or were they dining out that evening? *Dinner—dining out*—the old meaningless phraseology pursued her! She must try to think of herself as she would think of some one else, a some one dissociated from all the familiar routine of the past, whose wants and habits must gradually be learned, as one might spy out the ways of a strange animal …

The clock struck another hour—eleven. She stood up again and walked to the door: she thought she would go up stairs to her room. *Her* room? Again the word derided her. She opened the door, crossed the narrow hall, and walked up the stairs. As she passed, she noticed Westall's sticks and umbrellas: a pair of his gloves lay on the hall table. The same stair-carpet mounted between the same walls; the same old French print, in its narrow black frame, faced her on the landing. This visual continuity was intolerable. Within, a gaping chasm; without, the same untroubled and familiar surface. She must get away from it before she could attempt to think. But, once in her room, she sat down on the lounge, a stupor creeping over her …

Gradually her vision cleared. A great deal had happened in the interval—a wild marching and countermarching of emotions, arguments, ideas—a fury of insurgent impulses that fell back spent upon themselves. She had tried, at first, to rally, to organize these chaotic forces. There must be help somewhere, if only she could master the inner tumult. Life could not be broken off short like this, for a whim, a fancy; the law itself would side with her, would defend her. The law? What claim had she upon it? She was the prisoner of her own choice: she had been her own legislator, and she was the predestined victim of the code she had devised. But this was grotesque, intolerable—a mad mistake, for which she could not be held accountable! The law she had despised was still there, might still be invoked … invoked, but to what end? Could she ask it to chain Westall to her side? *She* had been allowed to go free when she claimed her freedom—should she show less magnanimity than she had exacted? Magnanimity? The word lashed her with its irony—one does not strike an attitude when one is fighting for life! She would threaten, grovel, cajole … she would yield anything to keep her hold on happiness. Ah, but the difficulty lay deeper! The law could not help her—her own apostasy could not help her. She was the victim of the theories she renounced. It was as though some giant machine of her own making had caught her up in its wheels and was grinding her to atoms …

It was afternoon when she found herself out-of-doors. She walked with an aimless haste, fearing to meet familiar faces. The day was radiant, metallic: one of those searching American days so calculated to reveal the shortcomings of our street-cleaning and the excesses of our architecture. The streets looked bare and hideous; everything stared and glittered. She called a passing hansom, and gave Mrs. Van Sideren's address. She did not know what had led up to the act; but she found herself suddenly resolved to speak, to cry out a warning. It was too late to save herself—but the girl might still be told. The hansom rattled up Fifth Avenue; she sat with her eyes fixed, avoiding recognition. At the Van Siderens' door she sprang out and rang the bell. Action had cleared her brain, and she felt calm and self-possessed. She knew now exactly what she meant to say.

The ladies were both out … the parlor-maid stood waiting for a card. Julia, with a vague murmur, turned away from the door and lingered a moment on the sidewalk. Then she remembered that she had not paid the cab-driver. She drew a dollar from her purse and handed it to him. He touched his hat and drove off, leaving her alone in the long empty street. She wandered away westward, toward strange thoroughfares, where she was not likely to meet acquaintances. The feeling of aimlessness had returned. Once she found herself in the afternoon torrent of Broadway, swept past tawdry shops and flaming theatrical posters, with a succession of meaningless faces gliding by in the opposite direction …

A feeling of faintness reminded her that she had not eaten since morning. She turned into a side street of shabby houses, with rows of ash-barrels behind bent area railings. In a basement window she saw the sign *Ladies' Restaurant:* a pie and a dish of doughnuts lay against the dusty pane like petrified food in an ethnological museum. She entered, and a young woman with a weak mouth and a brazen eye cleared a table for her near the window. The table was covered with a red and white cotton cloth and adorned with a bunch of celery in a thick tumbler and a salt-cellar full of grayish lumpy salt. Julia ordered tea, and sat a long time waiting for it. She was glad to be away from the noise and confusion of the streets. The low-ceilinged room was empty, and two or three waitresses with thin pert faces lounged in the background staring at her and whispering together. At last the tea was brought in a discolored metal teapot. Julia poured a cup and drank it hastily. It was black and bitter, but it flowed through her veins like an elixir. She was almost dizzy with exhilaration. Oh, how tired, how unutterably tired she had been!

She drank a second cup, blacker and bitterer, and now her mind was once more working clearly. She felt as vigorous, as decisive, as when she had stood on the Van Siderens' door-step—but the wish to return there had subsided. She saw now the futility of such an attempt—the humiliation to which it might have exposed her … The pity of it was that she did not know what to do next. The short winter day was fading, and she realized that she could not remain much longer in the restaurant without attracting notice. She paid for her tea and went out into the street. The lamps were alight, and here and there a basement shop cast an oblong of gas-light across the fissured pavement. In the dusk there was something sinister about the aspect of the street, and she hastened back toward Fifth Avenue. She was not used to being out alone at that hour.

At the corner of Fifth Avenue she paused and stood watching the stream of carriages. At last a policeman caught sight of her and signed to her that he would take her across. She had not meant to cross the street, but she obeyed automatically, and presently found herself on the farther corner. There she paused again for a moment; but she fancied the policeman was watching her, and this sent her hastening down the nearest side street … After that she walked a long time, vaguely … Night had fallen, and now and then, through the windows of a passing carriage, she caught the expanse of an evening waistcoat or the shimmer of an opera cloak …

Suddenly she found herself in a familiar street. She stood still a moment, breathing quickly. She had turned the corner without noticing whither it led; but now, a few yards ahead of her, she saw the house in which she had once lived—her first husband's house. The blinds were drawn, and only a faint translucence marked the windows and the transom above the door. As she stood there she heard a step behind her, and a man walked by in the direction of the house. He walked slowly, with a heavy middle-aged gait, his head sunk a little between the shoulders, the red crease of his neck visible above the fur collar of his overcoat. He crossed the street, went up the steps of the house, drew forth a latch-key, and let himself in …

There was no one else in sight. Julia leaned for a long time against the area-rail at the corner, her eyes fixed on the front of the house. The feeling of physical weariness had returned, but the strong tea still throbbed in her veins and lit her brain with an unnatural clearness. Presently she heard another step draw near, and moving quickly away, she too crossed the street and mounted the steps of the house. The impulse which had carried her there prolonged itself in a quick pressure of the electric bell—then she felt suddenly weak and tremulous, and grasped the balustrade for support. The door opened and a young footman with a fresh inexperienced face stood on the threshold. Julia knew in an instant that he would admit her.

"I saw Mr. Arment going in just now," she said. "Will you ask him to see me for a moment?"

The footman hesitated. "I think Mr. Arment has gone up to dress for dinner, madam."

Julia advanced into the hall. "I am sure he will see me—I will not detain him long," she said. She spoke quietly, authoritatively, in the tone which a good servant does not mistake. The footman had his hand on the drawing-room door.

"I will tell him, madam. What name, please?"

Julia trembled: she had not thought of that. "Merely say a lady," she returned carelessly.

The footman wavered and she fancied herself lost; but at that instant the door opened from within and John Arment stepped into the hall. He drew back sharply as he saw her, his florid face turning sallow with the shock; then the blood poured back to it, swelling the veins on his temples and reddening the lobes of his thick ears.

It was long since Julia had seen him, and she was startled at the change in his appearance. He had thickened, coarsened, settled down into the enclosing flesh. But she noted this insensibly: her one conscious thought was that, now she was face to face with him, she must not let him escape till he had heard her. Every pulse in her body throbbed with the urgency of her message.

She went up to him as he drew back. "I must speak to you," she said.

Arment hesitated, red and stammering. Julia glanced at the footman, and her look acted as a warning. The instinctive shrinking from a "scene" predominated over every other impulse, and Arment said slowly: "Will you come this way?"

He followed her into the drawing-room and closed the door. Julia, as she advanced, was vaguely aware that the room at least was unchanged: time had not mitigated its horrors. The contadina still lurched from the chimney-breast, and the Greek slave obstructed the threshold of the inner room. The place was alive with memories: they started out from every fold of the yellow satin curtains and glided between the angles of the rosewood furniture. But while some subordinate agency was carrying these impressions to her brain, her whole conscious effort was centred in the act of dominating Arment's will. The fear that he would refuse to hear her mounted like fever to her brain. She felt her purpose melt before it, words and arguments running into each other in the heat of her longing. For a moment her voice failed her, and she imagined herself thrust out before she could speak; but as she was struggling for a word, Arment pushed a chair forward, and said quietly: "You are not well."

The sound of his voice steadied her. It was neither kind nor unkind—a voice that suspended judgment, rather, awaiting unforeseen developments. She supported herself against the back of the chair and drew a deep breath. "Shall I send for something?" he continued, with a cold embarrassed politeness.

Julia raised an entreating hand. "No—no—thank you. I am quite well."

He paused midway toward the bell and turned on her. "Then may I ask—?"

"Yes," she interrupted him. "I came here because I wanted to see you. There is something I must tell you."

Arment continued to scrutinize her. "I am surprised at that," he said. "I should have supposed that any communication you may wish to make could have been made through our lawyers."

"Our lawyers!" She burst into a little laugh. "I don't think they could help me—this time."

Arment's face took on a barricaded look. "If there is any question of help—of course—"

It struck her, whimsically, that she had seen that look when some shabby devil called with a subscription-book. Perhaps he thought she wanted him to put his name down for so much in sympathy—or even in money … The thought made her laugh again. She saw his look change slowly to perplexity. All his facial changes were slow, and she remembered, suddenly, how it had once diverted her to shift that lumbering scenery with a word. For the first time it struck her that she had been cruel. "There *is* a question of help," she said in a softer key: "you can help me; but only by listening … I want to tell you something …"

Arment's resistance was not yielding. "Would it not be easier to—write?" he suggested.

She shook her head. "There is no time to write … and it won't take long." She raised her head and their eyes met. "My husband has left me," she said.

"Westall—?" he stammered, reddening again.

"Yes. This morning. Just as I left you. Because he was tired of me."

The words, uttered scarcely above a whisper, seemed to dilate to the limit of the room. Arment looked toward the door; then his embarrassed glance returned to Julia.

"I am very sorry," he said awkwardly.

"Thank you," she murmured.

"But I don't see—"

"No—but you will—in a moment. Won't you listen to me? Please!" Instinctively she had shifted her position putting herself between him and the door. "It happened this morning," she went on in short breathless phrases. "I never suspected anything—I thought we were—perfectly happy … Suddenly he told me he was tired of me … there is a girl he likes better … He has gone to her …" As she spoke, the lurking anguish rose upon her, possessing her once more to the exclusion of every other emotion. Her eyes ached, her throat swelled with it, and two painful tears burnt a way down her face.

Arment's constraint was increasing visibly. "This—this is very unfortunate," he began. "But I should say the law—"

"The law?" she echoed ironically. "When he asks for his freedom?"

"You are not obliged to give it."

"You were not obliged to give me mine—but you did."

He made a protesting gesture.

"You saw that the law couldn't help you—didn't you?" she went on. "That is what I see now. The law represents material rights—it can't go beyond. If we don't recognize an inner law … the obligation that love creates … being loved as well as loving … there is nothing to prevent our spreading ruin unhindered … is there?" She raised her head plaintively, with the look of a bewildered child. "That is what I see now ... what I wanted to tell you. He leaves me because he's tired ... but *I* was not tired; and I don't understand why he is. That's the dreadful part of it—the not understanding: I hadn't realized what it meant. But I've been thinking of it all day, and things have come back to me—things I hadn't noticed ... when you and I ..." She moved closer to him, and fixed her eyes on his with the gaze that tries to reach beyond words. "I see now that *you* didn't understand—did you?"

Their eyes met in a sudden shock of comprehension: a veil seemed to be lifted between them. Arment's lip trembled.

"No," he said, "I didn't understand."

She gave a little cry, almost of triumph. "I knew it! I knew it! You wondered—you tried to tell me—but no words came ... You saw your life falling in ruins ... the world slipping from you ... and you couldn't speak or move!"

She sank down on the chair against which she had been leaning. "Now I know—now I know," she repeated.

"I am very sorry for you," she heard Arment stammer.

She looked up quickly. "That's not what I came for. I don't want you to be sorry. I came to ask you to forgive me ... for not understanding that *you* didn't understand ... That's all I wanted to say." She rose with a vague sense that the end had come, and put out a groping hand toward the door.

Arment stood motionless. She turned to him with a faint smile.

"You forgive me?"

"There is nothing to forgive—"

"Then will you shake hands for good-by?" She felt his hand in hers: it was nerveless, reluctant.

"Good-by," she repeated. "I understand now."

She opened the door and passed out into the hall. As she did so, Arment took an impulsive step forward; but just then the footman, who was evidently alive to his obligations, advanced from the background to let her out. She heard Arment fall back. The footman threw open the door, and she found herself outside in the darkness.

MY FELLOW TRAVELLERS

Mary Angela Dickens

The room was the sitting-room of a ladies' residential flat. There were two people in it—a woman and a girl—ensconced in easy chairs, one on either side of the fire. The woman was the owner of the flat, and the girl had come up with her from the general dining-room after dinner, for coffee and conversation. Coffee was over, and upon the conversation one of those silences had fallen sometimes created by known and accepted differences of opinion.

The girl was leaning forward, gazing into the fire. She had straight features, redeemed from insignificance by the keen intelligence of their expression; but this intelligence in its turn, was rendered almost repellant by the exceeding hardness of its practicality. She looked pale and tired, and as a girl clerk is wont to do in the evening.

The woman also looked weary, as though she, too, had done a hard day's work. But in everything else the two countenances were sharply contrasted. The woman's was a strong face, and one that five and forty years of life might easily have rendered grim, but its dominant characteristic was a steady gentleness. The irregular features spoke not merely of intelligence, but of shrewd, well-developed brain power. She was leaning back in her chair, looking absently before her, when the girl spoke suddenly.

"Miss Lanyon," she said, "I don't understand you. You are so clever! You ought to be a materialist pure and simple. Your books are splendidly up to date in some ways, yet there is always that sad, old-fashioned, semi-Christian crank in them."

Apparently Miss Lanyon knew of something less offensive beneath the aggressive opinionativeness of the girlish personality for she answered with an odd little smile. Her voice was brisk and her utterance quick and decided.

"It's a great affliction to find oneself old-fashioned in these days," she said. "It is very kind of you not to despise me wholesale, Frances. As to materialism—well, I thought with you once upon a time. Ten years ago I fancy I should have satisfied you, altogether; and very little you would have liked me, if you did but know it."

The girl answered with a quick exclamation.

"You have been a materialist, then!" she exclaimed. "And you gave up certainties for these vague theories! Well, I must say that astonishes me!"

"I am glad to hear that you are capable of astonishment," was the quick, quaintly-uttered rejoinder. Then Miss Lanyon paused. She glanced at her companion's face, and spoke impulsively.

"I don't imagine it will make the slightest impression on you," she said. "Second-hand experiences are never of the faintest use. But I will tell you of something that happened to me ten years ago. Mind, I don't say that my present opinions, whatever they may be, are the direct outcome of that experience. Never mind now how opinions develop; you'll know some day. It simply showed me that materialism, at any rate, wouldn't do—that there was a vast tract of country which it failed to take into account. Would you like to hear about it?"

Hardly waiting for the girl's quick assent, leaning back in her chair with something about her whole figure, even in the uncertain light of the shaded lamp a trifle tense, Miss Lanyon began to speak again.

"Ten years ago," she said "I had not taken to writing books, and was a mistress in the High School at Norwich. I am not an imaginative woman, and in those days I held all the views most eminently qualified to stultifying such a quality. A woman devoid of any spiritual sense, without faith, and without romance, very seldom a pleasant creature. I was a conspicuously unpleasant specimen of the type, I imagine that is to say, I was as hard and self-satisfied as the most advanced woman need wish to be.

"It was the middle of the Christmas term. I had come up to town on a Saturday afternoon on business, and was returning to Norwich on Sunday evening. My train was to leave Liverpool Street at 6.15, and my brother, at whose house I had been staying, considered it his duty to go with me to the station.

"We had no time to spare when we reached Liverpool Street. I had a return ticket, and only a hand-bag by way of luggage, and we went straight through to the platform. I was travelling first class—a favourite extravagance of mine in these days—and we walked up the train to look for a carriage.

"As it was Sunday night, few people were travelling; but, on the other hand, few first-class compartments were provided. We looked into several, only to find that my favourite corners facing the engine were occupied, until we had almost reached the top of the train.

“The third carriage from the engine was a first, but I had noticed two or three people, after glancing into it, hesitate, and then pass down the train. Consequently, I was not surprised to see my brother, who was a few steps in front of me, pass it also, almost without looking into it. I was very much surprised however, when I passed it myself, to see that it was absolutely empty. I stopped, and called to my brother.

“‘Where are your eyes, Edward?’ I said. ‘This carriage is just the thing. It’s empty.’

“He turned back with a kind of vague dissatisfaction on his face.

“‘Is it?’ he said. ‘Oh, I suppose it’s all right then.’

“I had opened the door by that time, and, as he still hesitated, I got in. I did not take the corner nearest the door by which I had entered, as one naturally does, but I went instinctively, and without thinking about it, to the other end. I put down my book and umbrella on the seat there, and then my brother got in with my bag. He made no comment on my choice of a seat, and got out again rather quickly.

“‘Awfully stuffy carriage,’ he said.

“A scathing reply was on the tip of my tongue, when I became aware of the approach of a porter with footwarmers, and directed his attention to him.

“‘Put one in here,’ I said. ‘The further end.’

“The man did so. He paused a moment, and put another tin into the carriage, close to the open door.

“‘I suppose he thinks that you are going too,’ I remarked to Edward, as the man moved away.

“He answered rather absently.

“‘Yes, I suppose so,’ he said. ‘Are you quite sure—’

"The ringing bell interrupted him, and in another moment the train was moving slowly out of the station. I arranged my possessions to my liking, tucked myself up in my rug, and took up the book with which I intended to beguile the time, looking forward to a fairly pleasant journey.

"My book was one in which I had expected to be considerably interested, and I was rather annoyed when it gradually dawned upon me that it was not absorbing my attention in the least. I hardly seemed to take in, or to care to take in, what I read, and a feeling of vague dissatisfaction, utterly objectless and unreasonable, was stealing in and poisoning my contentment.

"Certainly, the weather was disagreeable. The wind was rising as we got into the country, and it howled and shrieked about the train as it pursued its rapid way. But I am not usually affected by such influences, and it surprised me considerably to think that the contrast between the clamour outside and the dead stillness within the carriage had no power to distract me. I found myself growing actually restless at last, and I thought it was time to concentrate my attention forcibly on my book. I made myself thoroughly comfortable, turning away from the empty carriage towards the window by which I was sitting, and propping one elbow on the ledge.

"I suppose I made myself too comfortable, for I went to sleep. I woke suddenly, opening my eyes with a full consciousness of my surroundings, and, as I did so, I was amazed to think that I must have slept for some time. I was in exactly the same position as that in which I had settled myself to read, and my eyes had opened directly upon the window. The train was evidently passing through some kind of cutting, and in the window the other end of the compartment was distinctly reflected.

"It was that which the reflection showed me that made me realise how heavily I had been sleeping, for it witnessed to the fact that we must have stopped, unknown to me, at a station. The carriage as pictured in the window, was no longer occupied only by myself. In the corner seats, on either side of the other door, were reflected the figures of a man and a woman.

"I did not turn round, partly through that curious notion of courtesy which dictates the ignoring of one's fellow travellers, partly because there was something rather interesting about the appearance of these particular people, and I was idly pleased to be able to study them by means of their reflections, without being guilty of actually staring at them.

"The corner seat obliquely facing me was occupied by the man. He was reading a newspaper, and only his forehead and the outline of his head were visible to me. He had taken off his hat, and his hair appeared to be fair and crisply curling. His figure was well made, and his pose spoke of self-possession and determination. There was, indeed, something almost excessively determined in the touch with which his hand held his paper. He was a gentleman, evidently, well appointed in every particular.

"It is difficult to account for the impression conveyed by appearance only—especially by an appearance seen merely as a reflection—but it was equally obvious to me that his companion belonged to a somewhat lower social grade.

"She was a girl of about nineteen, very tenderly and prettily made. The profile was charming; the small, delicately-cut features were full of expression. But there was a strained, painfully anxious look about them now, as she leaned forward, apparently talking eagerly to the man, and I found myself regretting that the noise of the train, and the shrieking of the wind—which had increased extraordinarily—should prevent my catching even the faintest sound of her voice. Arguing from something unusually dainty about her attire, from something essentially un-English about her face, and from the rapid and plentiful gestures with which she emphasised her speech, I settled in my own mind that she was French.

"I was watching her with a sense of growing fascination, when the conditions outside suddenly changed. The window ceased to act as a reflector. In place of the picture at which I had been looking the lights of a station flashed, and the train came to a standstill.

"The carriage had grown bitterly cold, and at the same time there was something curiously oppressive about the atmosphere. The door on my side opened on to the platform, and I sprang up—still without looking round—and let down the window with an irresistible impulse. I accounted to myself for the haste with which I had moved by looking eagerly for a porter with fresh foot warmers. No such person was visible, but nevertheless I did not draw in my head again.

"The groups of people moving to and fro had a singular attraction for me, and I stood there, at the window, in spite of the cold—which affected me less now that the window was open than it had done when it was shut—until the train began to move again. I sat down in my corner, pulled up the window, and then turned, for the first time since I had become aware of their presence, towards my fellow-travellers.

"The corner seats were vacant! They were no longer there!

"My first feeling, as I realised that I was alone, was one of blank astonishment. It is by no means usual for a train so to run into a station that passengers can get out from either side of a carriage. Moreover, not the slightest sound of their departure had reached my ears as I stood at the window. My astonishment subsided, however. I accepted the practical explanation of the matter which alone presented itself to me, and proceeded to compose myself once more to the enjoyment of my solitude.

"But for the first time in my life, solitude failed to make itself congenial to me. The brief interval of companionship—as conveyed by the contemplation and reflection of my fellow-travellers—had apparently demoralised me. A singular realisation of the isolation of my position, shut in there alone, and moving rapidly through the darkness, presented itself to me.

"The personality of those same fellow-travellers, also, had impressed me altogether unduly. It was not only that I could not forget them; I found myself dwelling on them. The girl's face came between me and the book I was reading; the man's callous indifference to her evident pleading oppressed me strangely. Vague sentences, the sense of which invariably eluded me as I tried to grasp them, kept floating through my mind, and I knew that I was trying to construct the drift of her words—those words of which I had not caught the faintest murmur.

"So completely possessed was I with the thought of the two that it did not strike me as being strange, when I gradually became aware of that singular feeling which everyone has experienced—the feeling that I was not alone. But I was distinctly surprised when I realised that the feeling was becoming curiously distasteful to me.

"It was absolutely still in the carriage, and, after the cheery bustle of the station, the quiet jarred on me. The beat and rumble of the train seemed to come from a long way off, shutting in the island of dead silence, of which I was the centre.

"I lifted my eyes from my book, on which they had been mechanically fixed, and looked about me. The dim lamp cast the usual depressing light over the usual accessories of a first-class carriage. Opposite me were the three empty places, divided by the regulation cushioned arms. On the side on which I sat were two more empty places. Between the two seats at the other end lay the unused footwarmer. It chimed in too aptly with my weird sense of unseen fellow-travellers, and pinching myself slightly, I turned with a sharp movement of self-contempt, to look out of the window at my side.

"I looked once more, not out into a dimly discerned landscape but into a clear-cut reflection of the carriage in which I sat. And there, reflected back with ghastly distinctness—reflected back as sitting in those seats which I had seen the instant before were empty—were my fellow-travellers."

Miss Lanyon paused. She was looking straight before her, her hands clenched tightly round the arms of her chair. Every trace of colour had died out of her strong face, and she went on in a slow harsh voice,

"You think you know what it is to be cold. Frances," she said. "You don't. You had better pray that you never may! It is to feel yourself gradually losing all human sensation; to feel that where there should be glowing moving blood there is motionless ice; to feel that the very atmosphere about you is not the atmosphere of every day, warm with the breath of your fellow creatures, but something rarified until its chill is agony.

"It comes about slowly—very, very slowly. First your heart ceases to beat—dies, and grows cold within you. Then the same cold spreads, little by little, until your every limb is frozen, and you can neither move nor breathe. I have felt cold only once in my life. I felt it then. I sat in my place, spell-bound, gazing at the reflection of that which I knew possessed no actual form, and the train swayed and jarred on its rushing way through the night.

"The position of the two figures had altered slightly. The man had laid down his paper, and his face was fully visible to me. It was the handsome face of a man of about thirty-five, blasé, and sensual in expression, and with a suggestion of cruelty about its lines.

"All its worst points were evidently accentuated at the moment. The brows were heavily contracted, and the mouth was very hard. The wind had dropped, suddenly. The throbbing beat of the train went on, rapid, monotonous, unceasing. There was absolute silence in the carriage. No external sounds came between my sense of hearing and the sound of a voice. But though I saw that he was speaking, I heard nothing.

"He was speaking sharply and decisively—that I saw. The girl was listening to him, her eyes fixed on his face, one hand pressed against her heart. It was her left hand, and ungloved, and I saw that it was ringless. Almost before he stopped she had broken again into speech. She was evidently dissenting from what he had said, trembling from head to foot with the vehemence of her emotion. Demonstrating, denying, pleading, the quivering passion threatening every moment to break through the difficult restraint of her expression, she lifted one small hand with a tremulous gesture, and, pushing the hair from her forehead, looked feverishly round the carriage.

"Her face was turned towards me, and I saw her eyes. Deep and dark, half wild, and desperate, I met them fully reflected in the glass, and in the same instant my own natural life, frozen and dead within me, seemed to be replaced by another. A burning, craving desire swelled up in me. I was shaken from head to foot by such an intensity of emotion as I had never known—as was utterly foreign to my temperament. As I sat there, conscious with a ghastly double consciousness of my own rigid, spell-bound figure, I knew that my agony of mind belonged not to me, but to her—to the girl reflected in the glass before me.

"She paused at last in her rapid speech, and such a sick hunger of hope and fear rose in my heart as almost choked me, while she waited, leaning rather forward, for his answer. There was a moment's pause. The wind shrieked and wailed, and my eyes burned in their sockets as I strained them upon the window. Then, without a word, the man took up his newspaper again.

"On the instant the girl started to her feet, tearing the newspaper from his hands, and facing him, her slender figure tense with fury. A passionate sense of intolerable wrong, of treachery and deceit, culminating in unendurable cruelty, was turning her brain to fire, and I watched, my very life seeming to beat in her frenzied, impulsive movements.

"Speaking wildly, almost incoherently, she lifted her hands to the throat of her dress, and drew out a little bit of ribbon, on which was strung a ring—a wedding ring. She dragged it off, snapping the ribbon-like cotton, and thrust the ring into its place on her finger, stretching out her left hand—the hand now of a wife—to him, as she did so, with a gesture which was superb in its agony and appeal. He did not move or speak; he was watching her with a heavy, lowering face; and as I looked from her to him I thought that if I had been free to talk or feel, I should have felt a shock of fear.

"Then, as suddenly as it had arisen, her form died away. Before I realised the change, she had fallen on her knees on the carriage floor, catching his hand in hers in such utter self-abandonment as I had never before conceived. I had heard of supplication, but I had never known what it meant until I shared the prayer which that unhappy girl raised to the man at whose feet she knelt.

"It was only for a moment. He drew his hand deliberately away, and, looking down into her upturned face, spoke one short sentence. For a moment the reflected figure of the girl knelt on there, motionless. Then she rose. She stood for an instance in silence, and then began to speak, slowly. He had driven her beyond the limits of endurance to defiance. She told him what she intended to do. I don't know what it was—I have never known—but I felt her meaning, then, as clearly as though I had heard her words. She drew from the bosom of her dress papers which she showed him as ocular demonstration of her intention, replacing them quietly.

"As he spoke I saw his face change. I saw the lines about his mouth contract. His hand moved rapidly to his breast pocket, the bright steel of a revolver flashed in the lamplight, and as I shrieked out in insane warning, the blackness of the night passed across the reflection, and I saw no more.

"The wind moaned, the throbbing beat of the train went on and on, and I sat there paralysed, staring straight before me, with burning, starting eyes. The darkness into which they looked was awful to me—the darkness which hid horror unspeakable.

"But the dimly-lighted carriage, on the other hand, was infinitely more awful. I dared not look round. The fearful conviction with which I was penetrated, that if I did so I should see nothing, was even more hideous to me than the ghastly companionship of which I was dimly conscious. The wild emotion of the past few moments had died out utterly. No feeling but one of sick, intolerable horror was alive in me as I waited, never turning my eyes, for what I knew would come.

"Many lifetimes of frozen suspense seemed to elapse, and then, suddenly, and without warning—as the necessary external conditions recurred—the reflection was visible again.

"I had known what I should see. I had thought that I was numbed to any further sense of horror. But as my eyes rested on the dreadful stillness of that girlish figure, huddled limply on the seat—beside me, as it were—I knew that I had been mistaken. At first I saw that figure only. My head was growing giddy, and I was on the verge of losing consciousness, when a stealthy movement in the reflection shocked me back to life. The man, who had been withdrawn out of range of the reflector, came back into the picture.

"He was white to the lips, and the evil determination of his face was hideous to see. I felt myself shrink and cower in my corner as though I were trying to hide from his wicked eyes. He stood still, and drew out his watch. Stepping with a care intolerable in its ghastly significance, he passed the motionless body, and going to the window, let it down and looked out. Then he pulled it up again, and began to move about with quick decisive movements.

"He took down his Gladstone from the rack, and unstrapped a second rug. Without an instant's pause, he lifted the heavy, inanimate form, and placed it carefully in the corner. With the same rapid, callous movements, he drew from the dead girl's dress the papers with which she had threatened him. One rug he arranged about her so as to give the impression of a sleeping figure; the other he flung on the floor at her feet, where it looked as though it had slipped from her knees. He put on his hat, and took his bag in his hand.

"By this time I knew we were slackening speed, slackening it slowly, and with the deliberation incidental to arrival at a large station. I felt that in a moment more the reflection must cease. We were going slower and slower. I saw the man put his hand on the handle of the door, turn it, and stand waiting. I saw him jump out, and then—the lights of a station once more, and the train at a standstill.

"I was released. I knew nothing else. An insane desire to see that cruel deed avenged, to bring down justice on the doer, literally possessed me. I rushed across the carriage, flung open the door, and, clutching at the first person I saw, entreated him wildly to stop the murderer, to fetch a doctor, not to let him go. I was vaguely aware of a circle of bewildered faces about me. I heard my voice rise to a hoarse cry, and then I fainted."

Miss Lanyon's voice ceased abruptly, and there was an interval of dead silence. She had spoken in a low, vibrating voice, the very intense restraint of which witnessed, as no words could have done, to the strength of her feelings. Her breath was coming thick and short. The girl who had listened to her was very still; her fingers were clenched tightly together in her lap, and she was rather pale. It was Miss Lanyon who spoke first.

"That's all," she said. "Don't take the trouble to comment, Frances. I know all the stock observations as to optical delusions, overstrung nerves, and dreams. Only I myself can realise the awful reality of that ghastly experience. I don't expect to convey it to anyone else."

"Did you ever find out—did you ever hear of any reason?" The girl's voice was low and awestruck. The manner with which Miss Lanyon had told her story had affected even her self-assured practicality.

There was a moment's pause, and then Miss Lanyon said, hoarsely:

"I found out, with infinite difficulty, that the dead body of a girl, shot through the heart, had been taken out of the train which reached Norwich at the same time in the evening, on the same day of the same month two years before. I heard that no clue to her identity had ever been discovered, and that her murderer had never been traced. And I heard that she had been found in the carriage occupying the same position on the train as that in which I had travelled from London—the third from the engine."

A low inarticulate exclamation broke from the girl, and then she was silent again. She was evidently making a valiant stand against the impression made on her, when she said, with rather uncertain assurance:

"It's a most curious story, Miss Lanyon, and I'm immensely grateful to you for telling it me. All the same, I don't see—"

Miss Lanyon interrupted her brusquely.

"No," she said. "But I did see. That is just the difference."

THE WOMAN WHO WAS SO TIRED

ELIZABETH BANKS

The assistant-editor wanted a story with "human interest" in it, so he looked around for the Little Reporter.

She came whirling in on the wings of the revolving door, dancing on her toes to keep up a circulation, her fingers wiggling within her muff, her veil dotted with frozen breath and tear-drops.

"My! It's cold!" she piped, "and so glassy, I slipped twice getting here from the elevated."

Throwing her frosted muff and coat on her roll-top desk, she lovingly hugged the radiator, holding in her half-numbed fingers the morning paper, while she scanned the head-lines.

They called her the "Little Reporter" because she was no bigger than your thumb, and because she belonged to that particular type of woman which always appeals to the male heart as needing to be taken care of.

"Yes," said the assistant-editor, "it is cold, and the weather has made me think of a story for you. New York must be full of suffering of one kind and another on a day like this. Just go out and spend it looking for the coldest woman in New York, or the saddest woman, or the most overworked woman, or the most anything woman in New York, and come back and write a story about her."

So the Little Reporter drew on her coat again and dried her veil and wrapped it about her face, and skipped blithely out by the circling door into the sleet, and late that night she limped back again and sat at her desk and wrote a story, and she called it "The Woman who was so Tired."

While the assistant-editor read the copy, it was noticed that he used his handkerchief freely, while swearing at whoever it might be who insisted upon fresh air from an open window.

"And me coming down with this cold in my head!" muttered the assistant-editor unsteadily.

The story of "The Woman who was so Tired" made a hit. It was full of a gay humour and a tender pathos that touched the heart. In it the Little Reporter seemed to have given her readers of her best, that best which made the smile break through the shining tears like a sun-burst through an April shower. People read, and as they read they laughed with "The Woman who was so Tired" at the comedies in her daily life, while as quickly they wept over her tragedies.

"The Woman who was so Tired" was described as young and self-supporting, and others-supporting as well, for she had a mother who stopped at home and kept the flat between intervals of pain, two little sisters in the graded school, and a young brother.

To earn their several livings "The Woman who was so Tired" had chosen a profession which made of her a wanderer in New York's streets, among the rich, the poor, the moderately well-to-do. Did not one know without a telling that she was a book canvasser or a seller of small wares at open doors—doors that so often shut in her face ere she had stated her errand?

All day she wandered among down-town offices, East-side tenements, West-side apartments. Sometimes into shops on Fifth Avenue and Broadway, sometimes into those of humble, dirty side-streets; sometimes she searched for treasure among the garbage cans. There were days when, in connection with her own legitimate business, she would attempt to aid those who were in greater distress than herself, and on certain of these days there were high-pitched voices that assailed her, and brooms held in filthy hands would almost sweep her down a squalid five flights of stairs. The longer she worked the better she was paid, for she worked not on a salary basis but on a commission.

Often when in the worst neighbourhoods of the East-side she would go hungry all the day, not because she lacked the pennies for food, but because her capricious appetite revolted against the fare served in any of the near-by restaurants.

She was often running to catch cars and trains, for minutes were precious to her; and she sometimes walked, seeking out her patrons, so she was always weary, and in writing of her the Little Reporter had named her "The Woman who was so Tired."

At the newspaper office they knew at once the story had made a hit, because it brought in letters by the dozens. Kind-hearted philanthropists demanded to be given the real name and address of "The Woman who was so Tired," for they knew she lived and moved among them every day, and that the author of the story had met her and known her well. She had gone to their hearts, and they wanted to do something for her. One saw the weary woman was proud, though poor, so the philanthropists declared they would help her without her knowing whence help came. New York working-women wrote, thanking the author for her championship of women who had to work overtime, for the heroine had been described as often working sixteen hours a day.

Before the end of a week the volume of correspondence concerning the story and its heroine so increased that now the Little Reporter had it heaped upon her desk in stacks, and presents began to arrive addressed to "The Woman who was so Tired" in care of the editor or the writer of the story. Cheques came in, and the Little Reporter often gashed the palm of her hand with the pins that fastened dollar bills to notepaper on which was daintily written or ignorantly scrawled a word of sympathy for the heroine of roving feet.

There were presents of warm clothing, dress-lengths, toys of various kinds for the little sisters and brother; a thin Coalport cup and saucer for the invalid mother who, in the story, was always longing for the dainty surroundings of better days; there were books, some grave, some laughter-giving, all nicely bound; boxes of chocolates, packages of nuts.

Very frequently now the assistant-editor would be called to the telephone to be asked for the address or further information of "The Woman who was so Tired," and he grew irritable over the continual interruptions to his work. "One might think," he said crossly, "that nobody ever was tired before and never would be again. Great Scot! I'm tired myself. Here!" he called to one of the office boys, "take this batch of letters and presents over to Miss Sanderson's desk, and tell her to call an expressman and forward 'em to that woman who was always tired!"

The Little Reporter looked up with a shrug of annoyance and protestation.

"Haven't ye got her address?" asked the boy sympathetically; then quickly he added, "Course not! She wouldn't give that, I guess, after all she told ye!"

They began to notice about the office that the Little Reporter in her corner was losing somewhat of her blithe look and manner. Her cheeks were paling, and her eyes saddened and took on the look that comes of little sleep. In and out of the office, then intermittently at her desk on which there now was scarce space for the moving of her pen, she worked on as was her custom, taking an assignment first here, then there, but her cheery laugh was now infrequent, and only occasionally now came a flash of wit in her hurried conversations with the different members of the staff. They tried to joke her about the heroine of her story, but she failed to respond with her old-time lightning-like repartee.

"So those cuts have come at last!" exclaimed the assistant-editor one afternoon, as a messenger boy bore toward him an oblong cardboard box. He stretched out his hands for it. For "The Woman who was so Tired. Please forward." This was the inscription on the attached label, and on the box, in gold letters, "Blank and Company, Florists, —, Broadway."

"Hang 'The Woman who was so Tired'!" he cried out angrily, then pointing to the desk where sat the Little Reporter, he added a bit softly, "Take 'em over to that lady."

She drew out from the box a dozen American Beauty roses, and hanging to the wide ribbon which bound their stems was a card. It read: "From a tired man to a tired woman."

She put them in the ice-water jug. They were beautiful roses and costly, and they shone out gloriously from among the heaps of parcels and letters addressed to "The Woman who was so Tired."

The Little Reporter's fingers trembled on her pencil, and a drop splashed down upon the yellow copy-paper. For a moment her hand pressed her temple, then she dropped her face in her hands. The assistant-editor walked over to her.

"Are you ill, Miss Sanderson?" he asked kindly.

"No-o-o," she drawled.

"I hope you haven't had bad news."

"No," she said again. "It's just about that Woman who was so Tired. It's on my conscience. I can't sleep—I—I—"

Nearly she broke down. Her eyes were growing bigger and rounder.

"All these letters, these bundles, these roses, oh! I didn't think it would turn out like this—how could I know people would go on so? I had to get a story. I couldn't waste all that time—I hunted and searched till nine o'clock that night, and I just—"

"It is useless for you to say you made it up," interrupted the assistant-editor. "I know it's true, everybody knows it's true!"

"I didn't make it up. It was all true—oh, don't you understand? I was IT!"

Her face went down among the roses and the parcels.

The assistant-editor gazed sturdily about the room, yet seeing none of the rush and the turmoil connected with getting out the next morning's paper, hearing none of the click of the typewriters nor the din of telegraph tables. And this was "The Woman who was so Tired." Their Little Reporter who went in and out among them, apparently so unconsciously cheerful, so full of the joy of life and work, calling out sometimes when she had finished two columns, "Find something else for me, so I can run up a nice space bill this week!"

His mind travelled over the details of the story that had stirred so many hearts. The woman had appeared to be a book-canvasser, working on commission—how like a reporter working on space and scouring the town for news! Frail and young, she had a whole family of dependants. In the story she had gone out in the ice and sleet, had slipped three times and turned her ankle. Instinctively he looked at the Little Reporter's feet and noticed that she was wearing odd boots, the one boot much larger than the other, doubtless because of the swelling of her strained ankle. Why, on the night of the day when he had sent her out, had she not returned laughing and limping?

He looked out of the window, out over the towering sky-scrapers of great New York, where daily he had sent her to bring in news of the city's joys and sorrows, its weddings and its funerals, its prayers and its cursings, its virtue and its vice, its feastings and its fasting. Great heavens! "The Woman who was so Tired" was often hungry! Had the Little Reporter ever lacked for food? Involuntarily his eye travelled back to her desk and rested upon the large-printed quotation one of the men reporters had jestingly hung above it the morning they had published her particularly racy and sparkling account of a banquet at Sherry's:

> "Who gives the fine report of the feast?
> She who got none and enjoyed it least!"

For three years now the Little Reporter had been on his staff, the one woman among a dozen men. He had hesitated about taking her on, she had seemed so tiny, so young, so irresponsible. She had never spoken of her family, her home. Who would have suspected the burden she carried so lightly upon her slight shoulders! And on the day he had sent her out to write of "the most anything woman" she could find in New York, surely there must have been some special reason at home why "good space" was necessary to her that day! Once he had laughingly called her an Oliver Twist, because she was always "asking for more" space. He had suspected she spent large sums for clothes, for she was always smartly dressed with stylish gowns and nobby hats, but the woman of her story made her own dresses and trimmed her hats on Sundays and after midnight! When did the Little Reporter get time to sleep?

From the high window he looked out again over busy, laughing, sorrowing, noisy, seething New York, then again at the head of the Little Reporter still sunk upon her desk, then around upon the men in the room.

"I expect," he thought, "we sometimes forget up here in our tower of observation that we too are a part of New York, and perhaps New York also forgets it. We're just a part, a part of it all, and how like we are, how very like!"

They were wanting him at his own desk, and he hurried over, yet turning an instant to look again at the Little Reporter and say a kindly word to reassure her troubled heart, he saw that her hand had fallen away from her face and that she was fast asleep in the midst of all the hubbub of the Press Room.

And he tripped off softly and motioned away young Bobbie, the office runner who was hurrying to her with proofs, lest he should disturb and awaken The Woman who was so Tired.

A CUP OF TEA

KATHERINE MANSFIELD

Rosemary Fell was not exactly beautiful. No, you couldn't have called her beautiful. Pretty? Well, if you took her to pieces. ... But why be so cruel as to take anyone to pieces? She was young, brilliant, extremely modern, exquisitely well dressed, amazingly well read in the newest of the new books, and her parties were the most delicious mixture of the really important people and ... artists—quaint creatures, discoveries of hers, some of them too terrifying for words, but others quite presentable and amusing.

Rosemary had been married two years. She had a duck of a boy. No, not Peter—Michael. And her husband absolutely adored her. They were rich, really rich, not just comfortably well off, which is odious and stuffy and sounds like one's grandparents. But if Rosemary wanted to shop she would go to Paris as you and I would go to Bond Street. If she wanted to buy flowers, the car pulled up at that perfect shop in Regent Street, and Rosemary inside the shop just gazed in her dazzled, rather exotic way, and said: "I want those and those and those. Give me four bunches of those. And that jar of roses. Yes, I'll have all the roses in the jar. No, no lilac. I hate lilac. It's got no shape." The attendant bowed and put the lilac out of sight, as though this was only too true; lilac was dreadfully shapeless. "Give me those stumpy little tulips. Those red and white ones." And she was followed to the car by a thin shopgirl staggering under an immense white paper armful that looked like a baby in long clothes. …

One winter afternoon she had been buying something in a little antique shop in Curzon Street. It was a shop she liked. For one thing, one usually had it to oneself. And then the man who kept it was ridiculously fond of serving her. He beamed whenever she came in. He clasped his hands; he was so gratified he could scarcely speak. Flattery, of course. All the same, there was something. …

"You see, madam," he would explain in his low respectful tones, "I love my things. I would rather not part with them than sell them to someone who does not appreciate them, who has not that fine feeling which is so rare. …" And, breathing deeply he unrolled a tiny square of blue velvet and pressed it on the glass counter with his pale finger-tips.

Today it was a little box. He had been keeping it for her. He had shown it to nobody as yet. An exquisite little enamel box with a glaze so fine it looked as though it had been baked in cream. On the lid a minute creature stood under a flowery tree, and a more minute creature still had her arms around his neck. Her hat, really no bigger than a geranium petal, hung from a branch; it had green ribbons. And there was a pink cloud like a watchful cherub floating above their heads. Rosemary took her hands out of her long gloves. She always took off her gloves to examine such things. Yes, she liked it very much. She loved it; it was a great duck. She must have it. And, turning the creamy box, opening and shutting it, she couldn't help noticing how charming her hands were against the blue velvet. The shopman, in some dim cavern of his mind, may have dared to think so too. For he took a pencil, leant over the counter, and his pale bloodless fingers crept timidly towards those rosy, flashing ones, as he murmured gently: "If I may venture to point out to madam, the flowers on the little lady's bodice."

"Charming!" Rosemary admired the flowers. But what was the price? For a moment the shopman did not seem to hear. Then a murmur reached her. "Twenty-eight guineas, madame."

"Twenty-eight guineas." Rosemary gave no sign. She laid the little box down; she buttoned her gloves again. Twenty-eight guineas. Even if one is rich. … She looked vague. She stared at a plump tea-kettle like a plump hen above the shopman's head, and her voice was dreamy as she answered: "Well, keep it for me—will you? I'll. …"

But the shopman had already bowed as though keeping it for her was all any human being could ask. He would be willing, of course, to keep it for her for ever.

The discreet door shut with a click. She was outside on the step, gazing at the winter afternoon. Rain was falling, and with the rain it seemed the dark came too, spinning down like ashes. There was a cold bitter taste in the air, and the new-lighted lamps looked sad. Sad were the lights in the houses opposite. Dimly they burned as if regretting something. And people hurried by, hidden under their hateful umbrellas. Rosemary felt a strange pang. She pressed her muff to her breast; she wished she had the little box, too, to cling to. Of course, the car was there. She'd only to cross the pavement. But still she waited. There are moments, horrible moments in life, when one emerges from shelter and looks out, and it's awful. One oughtn't to give way to them. One ought to go home and have an extra-special tea. But at the very instant of thinking that, a young girl, thin, dark, shadowy—where had she come from?—was standing at Rosemary's elbow and a voice like a sigh, almost like a sob, breathed: "Madame, may I speak to you a moment?"

"Speak to me?" Rosemary turned. She saw a little battered creature with enormous eyes, someone quite young, no older than herself, who clutched at her coat-collar with reddened hands, and shivered as though she had just come out of the water.

"M-madame," stammered the voice. "Would you let me have the price of a cup of tea?"

"A cup of tea?" There was something simple, sincere in that voice; it wasn't in the least the voice of a beggar. "Then have you no money at all?" asked Rosemary.

"None, madam," came the answer.

"How extraordinary!" Rosemary peered through the dusk, and the girl gazed back at her. How more than extraordinary! And suddenly it seemed to Rosemary such an adventure. It was like something out of a novel by Dostoevsky, this meeting in the dusk. Supposing she took the girl home? Supposing she did do one of those things she was always reading about or seeing on the stage, what would happen? It would be thrilling. And she heard herself saying afterwards to the amazement of her friends: "I simply took her home with me," as she stepped forward and said to that dim person beside her: "Come home to tea with me."

The girl drew back startled. She even stopped shivering for a moment. Rosemary put out a hand and touched her arm. "I mean it," she said, smiling. And she felt how simple and kind her smile was. "Why won't you? Do. Come home with me now in my car and have tea."

"You—you don't mean it, madam," said the girl, and there was pain in her voice.

"But I do," cried Rosemary. "I want you to. To please me. Come along."

The girl put her fingers to her lips and her eyes devoured Rosemary. "You're—you're not taking me to the police station?" she stammered.

"The police station!" Rosemary laughed out. "Why should I be so cruel? No, I only want to make you warm and to hear—anything you care to tell me."

Hungry people are easily led. The footman held the door of the car open, and a moment later they were skimming through the dusk.

"There!" said Rosemary. She had a feeling of triumph as she slipped her hand through the velvet strap. She could have said, "Now I've got you," as she gazed at the little captive she had netted. But of course she meant it kindly. Oh, more than kindly. She was going to prove to this girl that—wonderful things did happen in life, that—fairy godmothers were real, that—rich people had hearts, and that women *were* sisters. She turned impulsively, saying: "Don't be frightened. After all, why shouldn't you come back with me? We're both women. If I'm the more fortunate, you ought to expect. …"

But happily at that moment, for she didn't know how the sentence was going to end, the car stopped. The bell was rung, the door opened, and with a charming, protecting, almost embracing movement, Rosemary drew the other into the hall. Warmth, softness, light, a sweet scent, all those things so familiar to her she never even thought about them, she watched that other receive. It was fascinating. She was like the little rich girl in her nursery with all the cupboards to open, all the boxes to unpack.

"Come, come upstairs," said Rosemary, longing to begin to be generous. "Come up to my room." And, besides, she wanted to spare this poor little thing from being stared at by the servants; she decided as they mounted the stairs she would not even ring for Jeanne, but take off her things by herself. The great thing was to be natural!

And "There!" cried Rosemary again, as they reached her beautiful big bedroom with the curtains drawn, the fire leaping on her wonderful lacquer furniture, her gold cushions and the primrose and blue rugs.

The girl stood just inside the door; she seemed dazed. But Rosemary didn't mind that.

"Come and sit down," she cried, dragging her big chair up to the fire, "in this comfy chair. Come and get warm. You look so dreadfully cold."

"I daren't, madam," said the girl, and she edged backwards.

"Oh, please,"—Rosemary ran forward—"you mustn't be frightened, you mustn't, really. Sit down, and when I've taken off my things we shall go into the next room and have tea and be cosy. Why are you afraid?" And gently she half pushed the thin figure into its deep cradle.

But there was no answer. The girl stayed just as she had been put, with her hands by her sides and her mouth slightly open. To be quite sincere, she looked rather stupid. But Rosemary wouldn't acknowledge it. She leant over her, saying: "Won't you take off your hat? Your pretty hair is all wet. And one is so much more comfortable without a hat, isn't one?"

There was a whisper that sounded like "Very good, madam," and the crushed hat was taken off.

"Let me help you off with your coat, too," said Rosemary.

The girl stood up. But she held on to the chair with one hand and let Rosemary pull. It was quite an effort. The other scarcely helped her at all. She seemed to stagger like a child, and the thought came and went through Rosemary's mind, that if people wanted helping they must respond a little, just a little, otherwise it became very difficult indeed. And what was she to do with the coat now? She left it on the floor, and the hat too. She was just going to take a cigarette off the mantelpiece when the girl said quickly, but so lightly and strangely: "I'm very sorry, madam, but I'm going to faint. I shall go off, madam, if I don't have something."

"Good heavens, how thoughtless I am!" Rosemary rushed to the bell.

"Tea! Tea at once! And some brandy immediately!"

The maid was gone again, but the girl almost cried out. "No, I don't want no brandy. I never drink brandy. It's a cup of tea I want, madam." And she burst into tears.

It was a terrible and fascinating moment. Rosemary knelt beside her chair.

"Don't cry, poor little thing," she said. "Don't cry." And she gave the other her lace handkerchief. She really was touched beyond words. She put her arm round those thin, bird-like shoulders.

Now at last the other forgot to be shy, forgot everything except that they were both women, and gasped out: "I can't go on no longer like this. I can't bear it. I shall do away with myself. I can't bear no more."

"You shan't have to. I'll look after you. Don't cry any more. Don't you see what a good thing it was that you met me? We'll have tea and you'll tell me everything. And I shall arrange something. I promise. *Do* stop crying. It's so exhausting. Please!"

The other did stop just in time for Rosemary to get up before the tea came. She had the table placed between them. She plied the poor little creature with everything, all the sandwiches, all the bread and butter, and every time her cup was empty she filled it with tea, cream and sugar. People always said sugar was so nourishing. As for herself she didn't eat; she smoked and looked away tactfully so that the other should not be shy.

And really the effect of that slight meal was marvellous. When the tea-table was carried away a new being, a light, frail creature with tangled hair, dark lips, deep, lighted eyes, lay back in the big chair in a kind of sweet langour, looking at the blaze. Rosemary lit a fresh cigarette; it was time to begin.

"And when did you have your last meal?" she asked softly.

But at that moment the door-handle turned.

"Rosemary, may I come in?" It was Philip.

"Of course."

He came in. "Oh, I'm so sorry," he said, and stopped and stared.

"It's quite all right," said Rosemary smiling. "This is my friend, Miss—"

"Smith, madam," said the languid figure, who was strangely still and unafraid.

"Smith," said Rosemary. "We are going to have a little talk."

"Oh, yes," said Philip. "Quite," and his eye caught sight of the coat and hat on the floor. He came over to the fire and turned his back to it. "It's a beastly afternoon," he said curiously, still looking at that listless figure, looking at its hands and boots, and then at Rosemary again.

"Yes, isn't it?" said Rosemary enthusiastically. "Vile."

Philip smiled his charming smile. "As a matter of fact," said he, "I wanted you to come into the library for a moment. Would you? Will Miss Smith excuse us?"

The big eyes were raised to him, but Rosemary answered for her. "Of course she will." And they went out of the room together.

"I say," said Philip, when they were alone. "Explain. Who is she? What does it all mean?"

Rosemary, laughing, leaned against the door and said: "I picked her up in Curzon Street. Really. She's a real pick-up. She asked me for the price of a cup of tea, and I brought her home with me."

"But what on earth are you going to do with her?" cried Philip.

"Be nice to her," said Rosemary quickly. "Be frightfully nice to her. Look after her. I don't know how. We haven't talked yet. But show her—treat her—make her feel—"

"My darling girl," said Philip, "you're quite mad, you know. It simply can't be done."

"I knew you'd say that," retorted Rosemary. "Why not? I want to. Isn't that a reason? And besides, one's always reading about these things. I decided—"

"But," said Philip slowly, and he cut the end of a cigar, "she's so astonishingly pretty."

"Pretty?" Rosemary was so surprised that she blushed. "Do you think so? I—I hadn't thought about it."

"Good Lord!" Philip struck a match. "She's absolutely lovely. Look again, my child. I was bowled over when I came into your room just now. However … I think you're making a ghastly mistake. Sorry, darling, if I'm crude and all that. But let me know if Miss Smith is going to dine with us in time for me to look up *The Milliner's Gazette*."

"You absurd creature!" said Rosemary, and she went out of the library, but not back to her bedroom. She went to her writing-room and sat down at her desk. Pretty! Absolutely lovely! Bowled over! Her heart beat like a heavy bell. Pretty! Lovely! She drew her cheque book towards her. But no, cheques would be no use, of course. She opened a drawer and took out five pound notes, looked at them, put two back, and holding the three squeezed in her hand, she went back to her bedroom.

Half an hour later Philip was still in the library, when Rosemary came in.

"I only wanted to tell you," said she, and she leaned against the door again and looked at him with her dazzled exotic gaze, "Miss Smith won't dine with us tonight."

Philip put down the paper. "Oh, what's happened? Previous engagement?"

Rosemary came over and sat down on his knee. "She insisted on going," said she, "so I gave the poor little thing a present of money. I couldn't keep her against her will, could I?" she added softly.

Rosemary had just done her hair, darkened her eyes a little, and put on her pearls. She put up her hands and touched Philip's cheeks.

"Do you like me?" said she, and her tone, sweet, husky, troubled him.

"I like you awfully," he said, and he held her tighter. "Kiss me."

There was a pause.

Then Rosemary said dreamily, "I saw a fascinating little box today. It cost twenty-eight guineas. May I have it?"

Philip jumped her on his knee. "You may, little wasteful one," said he.

But that was not really what Rosemary wanted to say.

"Philip," she whispered, and she pressed his head against her bosom, "am I *pretty*?"

A MOTOR

Elizabeth Bibesco

There is a special quality about a December sunset. The ruffles of red-gold gradually untightening, the congested mauve islands on a transparent sea of green, the ultimate luminous primrose dissolving into violet powder and then the cold, biting night, lit up by strange patches of colour that have somehow been forgotten in the sky.

Eve was walking home, her quick, defiant movements challenging the evening, her head bent slightly forward, her chin almost touching her muff, while her eyes shone and her cheeks glowed and her lithe figure seemed almost to be cutting through the icy air.

"This is happiness," she thought exultantly, "this bitter winter stimulus—I feel so light—as if my heart and mind were empty—only my body is quivering with life—the pure life of physical fitness. Why think, or feel, or look forward?" She doubled her pace until her feet seemed to be skimming the road. "I feel like a duck and drake," she laughed to herself. "Nothing matters, nothing, while there is still frost in the world."

And then she saw a little motor waiting on the other side of the road. She stopped dead and her heart stopped with her.

"There is no reason why it should be his. Hundreds of people have motors like that."

Resolutely she took a step forward. "I can't see from here, and I won't go and look," she added as she crossed over.

And then, shutting her eyes:

"Jerry," she said to herself, trying to kill his ghost with his name.

The evening air had become damp and penetrating. It made her throat feel sore and she choked a little as she breathed it.

Gingerly she approached the motor to make sure. What an absurd phrase! Why, a leap of her heart would have announced its presence, even had her eyes been shut.

She knew its every detail, the sound the gears made changing, the feel of the seat, the way the hood went up. And, above all, the little clock, ticking its warning by day, regular and relentless, while, at night, its bright, prying eyes reminded her of all the things she wanted to forget. "It is my conscience," she would say, "and fate and mortality. It symbolizes all the limitations of life. It is the frontier to happiness, the defeat of peace."

"Go on," he had said, "and you will end by forgetting it."

It was what he had called her habit of "talking things away."

How often she had slipped into his motor after him, sliding along the shiny leather, nestling happily against him, explaining that there was no draught, that the rain was not coming in, that her feet were as warm as toast. How often he had steered slowly with one hand, while her fingers crept into the palm of the other. And then he had turned off the engine and they had sat there together silent and alone, cut off from the world. How she had loved his motor! Surreptitiously she would caress it with her hand, stroking the cool shiny leather, and, seeing him looking at her, she would say,

"I think my purse must have fallen behind the seat." It had become to her a child and a mother, a refuge and an adventure, an island cut off from all the wretched necessities of existence, associated only with her and with him. It was a much better kingdom than a room; for a room is full of paraphernalia and impedimenta, with books and photographs, and the envelopes of letters to remind you of people and things that you want to forget. After all she could not sweep her house clear of her life, empty it of the necessary and the superfluous of her ties and her duties and her responsibilities.

But his motor—his little gasping uncomfortable motor—that was really and truly hers, because it was his. Here was her throne and his altar.

No wonder she sometimes stroked it a little, when it was too dark for him to ask her what she was doing.

And now, now some one else crept in after him, slid towards him on the shiny leather, murmured that her feet were as warm as toast, that there was no draught, and of course the rain didn't come in …

Or did she say, "Do you think there is something the matter with your car to-day? It seems a little asthmatic."

Eve looked at the house. She could see brightness shining behind the curtains. She could imagine a glowing fire and a faint smell of warm roses. Who was the woman? What were they doing? Sitting on either side of the fireplace drowsily intimate, smiling a little perhaps and hardly talking, conscious only of the cold outside and the warm room and one another …

Eve shivered. Almost unconsciously she fingered the mud guard. "A room is a horrible, unprivate thing," she said. "People walk in and out of it, anyone, and there are books and photographs and letters. It is a market place, not a sanctuary—whereas you …" She looked at the little motor. It was too dark to see anything, but every line of it was branded on her heart.

"No one will ever love you as I did," she said to it, and slowly, wearily, dragging one foot after another, she walked away into the cold raw night.

"Nothing in the world like winter air to make you feel fit," Bob said to himself as he swung himself along the road at a tremendous pace.

"Jove, what a sunset!" he added, looking up at the red-gold ruffles slowly untightening. He reflected that there is nothing in the world like health. Live cleanly and the high thinking will look after itself—or at least won't matter. Physical fitness, there's nothing like it. Love and that sort of thing is all very well in its way, but a cold bath in the morning and plenty of exercise … He began to whistle, and then—because he did feel most frightfully well—to run.

"Run a mile without being out of breath," he thought complacently, and then—because he hadn't meant to—"wasn't even thinking of her" he grumbled to Providence—he found himself outside her door. And in the road there was a motor, a little coral-coloured motor. He looked at it in dismay and then he looked at the house. He saw it was lit up and he imagined the room he knew so well. The crimson damask curtains and the creamy walls, the glowing fire and the red roses, the roses he had sent for her. Probably she would be sitting on that white fur rug on the floor, her arms clasped round her knees, her red hair as bright as the red-hot coals, her dark eyes dreamy and half closed.

"Damn him, I wonder who he is," and he started examining the motor.

"It's not very new," he thought; "the varnish is all off and those shiny leather seats are damned cold and slippery, draughty too, I should say; hood doesn't close properly. Must let in the rain like a leaking boat."

He put his hand on the mud guard. "Bent." he said. He felt a little cheered. But then, looking at the glowing house, he grew disconsolate again.

"Wonder what they're doing," he grumbled to himself. "Jabbering away, I'll be bound. Never was much of a hand at talking myself. Wonder who the deuce he is."

And then he looked contemptuously at the little motor.

"Damned if I couldn't do her better than that," he said. "God, how cold it is."

Irresolutely he moved away. Then he began to run, but the raw air caught his throat and he felt out of breath.

"Not so young as I was," he thought as he walked away into the damp night.

ANN LEE'S

Elizabeth Bowen

Ann Lee's occupied a single frontage in one of the dimmer and more silent streets of south-west London. Grey-painted woodwork framed a window over which her legend was inscribed in far-apart black letters: "ANN LEE—HATS." In the window there were always just two hats; one on a stand, one lying on a cushion; and a black curtain with a violet border hung behind to make a background for the hats. In the two upper stories, perhaps, Ann Lee lived mysteriously, but this no known customer had ever inquired, and the black gauze curtains were impenetrable from without.

Mrs. Dick Logan and her friend Miss Ames approached the shop-front. Miss Ames had been here once before two years ago; the hat still existed and was frequently admired by her friends. It was she who was bringing Mrs. Dick Logan; she hesitated beneath the names at the street corner, wrinkled up her brows, and said she hadn't remembered that Ann Lee's was so far from Sloane Square Station. They were young women with faces of a similar pinkness; they used the same swear-words and knew the same men. Mrs. Dick Logan had decided to give up Clarice; her husband made such a ridiculous fuss about the bills and she had come to the conclusion, really, that considering what she had to put up with every quarter-day she might have something more to show for it in the way of hats. Miss Ames, who never dealt there, agreed that Clarice *was* expensive: now there was that shop she had been to once, Ann Lee's, not far from Sloane Street —

"Expensive?" Mrs. Dick said warily.

"Oh well, not cheap. But most emphatically worth it. You know, I got that green there—"

"O-oh," cried Mrs. Dick Logan, "that *expressive* green!"

So they went to find Ann Lee.

It was an afternoon in January, and their first sensation was of pleasure as they pushed open the curtained door and felt the warm air of the shop vibrate against their faces. An electric fire was reflected in a crimson patch upon the lustrous pile of the black carpet. There were two chairs, two mirrors, a divan and a curtain over an expectant archway. No hats were visible.

"Nice interior!" whispered Mrs. Logan.

"Very much *her*," returned Miss Ames. They loosened their furs luxuriously, and each one flashed sidelong at herself in a mirror an appraising glance. They had a sense of having been sent round on approval, and this deepened in the breast of Mrs. Logan as their waiting in the empty shop was prolonged by minute after minute. Clarice came rushing at one rather: Mrs. Logan was predisposed to like Ann Lee for her discreet indifference to custom. Letty Ames had said that she was practically a lady; a queer creature, Letty couldn't place her.

"I wonder if she realises we're here," whispered Letty, her brows again faintly wrinkled by proprietary concern. "We might just cough—not an angry cough, quite natural. You'd better, Lulu, 'cause you've got one."

Mrs. Logan really had a slight catarrh, and the sound came out explosively. They heard a door softly open and shut, and the sound of feet descending two or three carpeted steps. There was another silence, then close behind the curtain one cardboard box was placed upon another, and there was a long, soft, continuous rustling of tissue paper. One might almost have believed Ann Lee to be emerging from a bandbox. Then the curtain twitched, quivered, and swung sideways, and some one gravely regarded them a moment from the archway.

"Good afternoon," she said serenely, and "Good afternoon."

Her finger brushed a switch, and the shop became discreetly brilliant with long shafts of well-directed light.

"I've come back again," Miss Ames brought out a shade dramatically, and Ann Lee nodded. "Yes, so I see. I'm glad, Miss Ames. I had expected you." She smiled, and Mrs. Dick Logan felt chilly with exclusion. "And I've brought my friend, Mrs. Dick Logan."

Ann Lee, with delicately arched-up eyebrows, turned to smile.

She was slight and very tall, and the complete sufficiency of her unnoticeable dress made Mrs. Dick Logan feel gaudy. Her hands were long and fine, her outspread fingers shone against her dress—on a right-hand, non-committal finger she wore one slender ring. Her face was a serene one, the lips a shade austere, and her hair was closely swathed about her head in bright, sleek bands. There was something of the priestess about her, and she suffered their intrusion with a ceremonial grace. She was so unlike Clarice and all those other women, that Mrs. Logan hardly knew how to begin, and was gratified, though half-conscious of a solecism, when Miss Ames said, "My friend would like so much to see some hats. She's rather wanting two or three hats."

Ann Lee's eyes dwelt dispassionately on Mrs. Logan's face. She looked questioningly at the eyebrows and searchingly at the mouth, then said with an assumption that barely deferred to her customer, "Something quiet?"

Something quiet was the last thing Mrs. Logan wanted. She wanted something nice and bright to wear at Cannes, but she hardly liked to say so. She put forward timidly, "Well, not *too* quiet—it's for the Riviera."

"Really?" said Ann Lee regretfully—"how delightful for you to be going out. I don't know whether I have—no, wait; perhaps I have some little model."

"I rather thought a turban—gold, perhaps?"

"Oh, a *turban*—? But surely you would be more likely to find what you want out there? Surely Cannes—"

This made Mrs. Logan feel peevish. Even if a person did look like a Madonna or something, it was their business to sell a hat if they kept a shop for that purpose. She hadn't followed Letty quite endlessly through those miserable back streets to be sent away disdainfully and told to buy her hats in France. She didn't care for shopping on the Riviera, except with her Casino winnings; the shops expected to be paid so soon, and Dickie made an even worse fuss when he saw a bill in francs. She said querulously:

"Yes, but haven't you got anything of that sort? Any goldish, sort of turbany thing?"

"I never have many hats," said Ann Lee. "I will show you anything I have."

Lulu glanced across at Letty, breathing more deeply with relief at this concession, and Letty whispered, as Ann Lee vanished momentarily behind the curtain: "Oh, she's always like that; like what I told you, queer. But the *hats,* my dear! You wait!"

When Ann Lee returned again carrying two hats, Mrs. Logan admitted that there had indeed been something to wait for. These were the hats one dreamed about—no, even in a dream one had never directly beheld them; they glimmered rather on the margin of one's dreams. With trembling hands she reached out in Ann Lee's direction to receive them. Ann Lee smiled deprecatingly upon her and them, then went away to fetch some more.

Lulu Logan snatched off the hat she was wearing and let it slide unnoticed from the brocaded seat of the chair where she had flung it and bowl away across the floor. Letty snatched off hers too, out of sympathy, and, each one occupying a mirror, they tried on every single hat Ann Lee brought them; passing each one reverently and regretfully across to one another, as though they had been crowns. It was very solemn. Ann Lee stood against the curtain of the archway, looking at them gently and pitifully with her long pale eyes. Her hands hung down by her sides; she was not the sort of person who needs to finger the folds of a curtain, touch the back of a chair, or play with a necklace. If Mrs. Logan and her friend Miss Ames had had either eyes, minds, or taste for the comparison, they might have said that she seemed to grow from the floor like a lily. Their faces flushed; soon they were flaming in the insidious warmth of the shop. "Oh, *damn* my face!" groaned Miss Ames into the mirror, pressing her hands to her cheeks, looking out at herself crimsonly from beneath the trembling shadow of an osprey.

How could Lulu ever have imagined herself in a gold turban? In a gold turban, when there were hats like these? But she had never known that there were hats like these, though she had tried on hats in practically every shop in London that she considered fit to call a shop. Life was still to prove itself a thing of revelations, even for Mrs. Dick Logan. In a trembling voice she said that she would certainly have *this* one, and she thought she simply must have *this,* and "Give me back the blue one, darling!" she called across to Letty.

Then a sword of cold air stabbed into the shop, and Lulu and Letty jumped, exclaimed and shivered. The outer door was open and a man was standing on the threshold, blatant in the light against the foggy dusk behind him. Above the suave folds of his dazzling scarf his face was stung to scarlet by the cold; he stood there timid and aggressive; abject in his impulse to retreat, blustering in his determination to resist it. The two ladies stood at gaze in the classic pose of indignation of discovered nymphs. Then they both turned to Ann Lee, with a sense that something had been outraged that went deeper than chastity. The man was not a husband; he belonged to neither of them.

The intruder also looked towards Ann Lee; he dodged his head upwards and sideways in an effort to direct his line of vision past them. He opened his mouth as though he were going to shout; then they almost started at the small thin voice that crept from it to say "Good evening."

Ann Lee was balancing a toque upon the tips of her fingers, an imponderable thing of citron feathers, which even those light fingers hardly dared to touch. Not a feather quivered and not a shadow darkened her oval face as she replied, "Good evening," in a voice as equably unsmiling as her lips and eyes.

"I'm afraid I've come at a bad moment."

"Yes," she said serenely, "I'm afraid you have. It's quite impossible for me to see you now; I'm sorry—I believe that hat is *you,* Mrs. Logan. I'm sorry you don't care for black."

"Oh, I do like black," said Mrs. Logan unhappily, feasting upon her own reflection. "But I've got so many. Of course, they do set the face off, but I particularly wanted something rather sunny looking—now that little blue's perfect. How much did you ...?"

"Eight guineas," said Ann Lee, looking at her dreamily.

Mrs. Logan shivered and glanced vindictively towards the door. Ann Lee was bending to place the toque of citron feathers on the divan; she said mildly over her shoulder, with one slight upward movement of her lashes, "We are a little cold in here, if you don't mind."

"Sorry!" the man said, looking wildly into the shop. Then he came right in with one enormous step and pulled the door shut behind him. "I'll wait then, if I may." He looked too large, with his angular blue cloth overcoat double-buttoned across the chest, and as he stuffed his soft grey hat almost furtively under his arm they saw at once that there was something wrong about his hair. One supposed he couldn't help it waving like that, but he might have worn it shorter. The shoes on his big feet were very bright. Fancy a man like that ... Lulu allowed a note of injury to creep into her voice as she said, "I beg your pardon," and reached past him to receive another hat from Letty. The shop was quite crowded, all of a sudden. And really, walking in like that ... He didn't know what they mightn't have been trying on; so few shops nowadays were hats exclusively. He didn't see either herself or Letty, except as things to dodge his eyes past—obstacles. The way he was looking at Ann Lee was disgusting. A woman who asked eight guineas for a little simple hat like that blue one had got no right to expose her customers to this.

Letty, her hair all grotesquely ruffled up with trying-on, stood with a hat in either hand, her mouth half open, looking at the man not quite intelligently. One might almost have believed that she had met him. As a matter of fact, she was recognising him; not as his particular self but as an Incident. He—It—crops up periodically in the path of any young woman who has had a bit of a career, but Ann Lee—really. Letty was vague in her ideas of Vestal Virgins, but dimly she connected them with Ann. Well, you never knew. … Meanwhile this was a hat shop; the least fitting place on earth for the recurrence of an Incident. Perhaps it was the very priestliness of Ann which made them feel that there was something here to desecrate.

Ann Lee, holding the blue hat up before the eyes of Lulu, was the only one who did not see and tremble as the square man crossed the shop towards the fireplace and sat down on the divan beside the feather toque. He was very large. He drew his feet in with an obvious consciousness of offence and wrapped the skirts of his overcoat as uncontaminatingly as possible about his knees. His gaze crept about the figure of Ann. "I'll wait, if you don't mind," he repeated.

"I'm afraid it's no good," she said abstractedly, looking past him at the toque. "I'm busy at present, as you can see, and afterwards I've orders to attend to. I'm sorry. Hadn't you better—?"

"It's four o'clock," he said.

"Four o'clock!" shrieked Lulu. "Good God, I'm due at the Cottinghams!"

"Oh, don't go!" wailed Letty, whose afternoon was collapsing.

Ann Lee, smiling impartially, said she did think it was a pity not to decide.

"Yes, but eight guineas." It needed a certain time for decision.

"It's a lovely little hat," pleaded Letty, stroking the brim reverently.

"Yes, it's pretty," conceded Ann Lee, looking down under her lids at it with the faintest softening of the lips. They all drew together, bound by something tense: the man before the fire was forgotten.

"Oh, I don't know," wailed the distracted Mrs. Logan. "I must have that little black one, and I ought to get another dinner-hat— You know how one needs them out there!" she demanded of Miss Ames reproachfully. They both looked appealingly at Ann Lee. She was not the sort of person, somehow, that one could ask to reduce her things. There was a silence.

"It *is* four o'clock!" said the man in a bullying, nervous voice. They jumped. "You *did* say four o'clock," he repeated.

Ann Lee quite frightened the two others; she was so very gentle with him, and so scornfully unemphatic. "I'm afraid you are making a mistake. On Thursdays I am always busy. Good evening, Mr. Richardson; don't let us waste any more of your time. Now, Mrs. Logan, shall we say the blue? I feel that you would enjoy it, though I still think the black is a degree more *you.* But I daresay you would not care to take both."

"I'll wait," he said, in a queer voice. Unbuttoning his overcoat, he flung it open with a big, defiant gesture as he leaned towards the fire. "Oh, the *toque!*" they screamed; and Ann Lee darted down and forwards with a flashing movement to retrieve the frail thing from beneath the iron folds of the overcoat. She carried it away again on the tips of her fingers, peering down into the ruffled feathers; less now of the priestess than of the mother—Niobe, Rachel. She turned from the archway to say in a white voice, her face terrible with gentleness, "Then will you kindly wait outside?"

"It's cold," he pleaded, stretching out his hands to the fire. It was a gesture: he did not seem to feel the warmth.

"Then wouldn't it be better not to wait?" Ann Lee softly suggested.

"I'll wait to-day," he said, with bewildered and unshaken resolution. "I'm not going away *to-day.*"

While she was away behind the curtain, rustling softly in that world of tissue paper, the man turned from the fire to look round at the contents of the shop. He looked about him with a kind of cringing triumph, as one who has entered desecratingly into some Holiest of Holies and is immediately to pay the penalty, might look about him under the very downsweep of the sacerdotal blade. He noted without comment or emotion the chairs, the lustrous carpet, Mrs. Logan's hat, the ladies, and the mirrors opposite one another, which quadrupled the figure of each lady. One could only conclude that he considered Miss Ames and Mrs. Logan as part of the fittings of the shop—"customers" such as every shop kept two of among the mirrors and the chairs; disposed appropriately; symbolic, like the two dolls perpetually recumbent upon the drawing-room sofa of a doll's house. He stared thoughtfully at Miss Ames, not as she had ever before been stared at, but as though wondering why Ann Lee should have chosen to invest her shop with a customer of just *that* pattern. Miss Ames seemed for him to be the key to something; he puzzled up at her with knitted brows.

"Perhaps it would be better for us to be going?" said Miss Ames to Mrs. Logan, her words making an icy transition above the top of his head. "I'm afraid it's difficult for you to decide on anything with the place crowded and rather a lot of talking."

Mrs. Logan stood turning the blue hat round and round in her hands, looking down at it with tranced and avid eyes. "Eight—sixteen—twenty-four," she murmured. "I do think she might reduce that little toque. If she'd let me have the three for twenty-two guineas."

"Not she," said Letty with conviction.

The man suddenly conceded their humanity. "I suppose these are what you'd call expensive hats?" he said, looking up at Mrs. Logan.

"Very," said she.

"Several hundreds, I daresay, wouldn't buy up the contents of the shop, as it stands at present?"

"I suppose not," agreed Mrs. Logan, deeply bored—"Letty, when *is* she coming back? Does she always walk out of the shop like this? Because *I* call it ... I shall be so late at the Cottinghams, too. I'd be off this minute, but I just can't leave this little blue one. Where'll we get a taxi?"

"First corner," said the man, rearing up his head eagerly. "Round on your left."

"Oh, thanks," they said frigidly. He was encouraged by this to ask if they, too, didn't think it was very cold. Not, in fact, the sort of weather to turn a dog out. "I'm sorry if I've inconvenienced you any way by coming in, but I've an appointment fixed with Miss Lee for four o'clock, specially fixed, and you can imagine it was cold out there, waiting—" The rustling of the paper ceased; they thought the curtain twitched. He turned and almost ate the archway with his awful eyes. Nothing happened; the sleek heavy folds still hung down unshaken to the carpet. "I've an appointment," he repeated, and listened to the echo with satisfaction and a growing confidence. "But I don't mind waiting—I've done so much waiting."

"Really?" said Miss Ames, in the high voice of indifference. Determined that she must buy nothing, she was putting her own hat on again resignedly. "She's bound to be back in a jiff," she threw across reassuringly to Lulu, who sat bareheaded by a mirror, statuesquely meditative, her eyes small with the effort of calculation.

"I don't suppose either of you ladies," said the man tremendously, "have spent so much time in your whole lives trying on clothes in shops of this kind, as I've spent outside just this one shop, waiting. If any more ladies come in, they'll just have to take me naturally, for I'm going to sit on here where I am till closing time."

Miss Ames, fluffing her side hair out in front of the mirror, repeated "Really?" bland as a fish.

"I'm quite within my rights here," said he, looking down now with approval at his feet so deeply implanted in the carpet, "because you see, I've got an appointment."

"There was no appointment, Mr. Richardson," said Ann Lee regretfully, standing in the archway.

Mrs. Dick Logan, catching her breath, rose to her feet slowly, and said that she would have all three hats, and would Ann Lee send them along at once, please. It was an immense moment, and Miss Ames, who knew Dickie, thought as she heard Mrs. Logan give her name and address in a clear unfaltering voice that there *was* something splendid about Lulu. The way she went through it, quarter-day after quarter-day ... Miss Ames glowed for their common femininity as she watched her friend pick up yet another hat and try it on, exactly as if she could have had it too, if she had wished, and then another and another. Ann Lee, writing languidly in an order-book, bowed without comment to Mrs. Logan's decision. And Letty Ames couldn't help feeling also that if Ann Lee had wished, Lulu would have had that other hat, and then another and another.

Mrs. Logan stooped to recover her own hat from the floor. Ann Lee, looking down solicitously, but making no movement to assist her, meditated aloud that she was glad Mrs. Logan was taking that little black. It was so much *her*, to have left it behind would have been a pity, Ann Lee couldn't help thinking.

As they gathered their furs about them, drew on their gloves, snapped their bags shut, and nestled down their chins into their furs, the two ladies glanced as though into an arena at the man sitting on the divan, who now leaned forwards to the fire again, his squared back towards them. And now? They longed suddenly, ah, how they longed, to linger in that shop.

"Good afternoon," said Ann Lee. She said it with finality.

"Good afternoon," they said, still arrested a second in the doorway. As they went out into the street reluctantly they saw Ann Lee, after a last dim bow towards them, pass back through the archway so gently that she scarcely stirred the curtains. The man beside the fire shot to his feet, crossed the shop darkly, and went through after her, his back broad with resolution.

There were no taxis where they had been promised to find them, and the two walked on in the direction of Sloane Street through the thickening fog. Mrs. Dick Logan said that she didn't think she dared show her face at the Cottinghams now, but that really those hats were worth it. She walked fast and talked faster, and Miss Ames knew that she was determined not to think of Dickie.

When they came to the third corner they once more hesitated, and again lamented the non-appearance of a taxi. Down as much of the two streets as was visible, small shop-windows threw out squares of light on to the fog. Was there, behind all these windows, some one waiting, as indifferent as a magnet, for one to come in? "What an extraordinary place it was," said Mrs. Logan for the third time, retrospectively. "How she ever sells her things ..."

"But she does sell them."

"Yes." She did sell them, Mrs. Logan knew.

As they stood on the kerbstone, recoiling not without complaints from the unkindness of the weather, they heard rapid steps approaching them, metallic on the pavement, in little uneven spurts of speed. Somebody, half blinded by the fog, in flight from somebody else. They said nothing to each other, but held their breaths, mute with a common expectancy.

A square man, sunk deep into an overcoat, scudded across their patch of visibility. By putting out a hand they could have touched him. He went by them blindly; his breath sobbed and panted. It was by his breath that they knew how terrible it had been—terrible.

Passing them quite blindly, he stabbed his way on into the fog.

THE SNOWSTORM

Violet M. MacDonald

Elizabeth read half-way through the letter, then stopped, dropped her hand on her knee and laughed aloud. She read again from the beginning and stopped as before, laughed as before, and then frowned. She read on to the end, her mood turning from incredulity to anger, then to fear, then to curiosity and a faint sense of excitement. She was completely bewildered.

"The man's mad," she said.

Months before, in the summer, she had been ferreting about in the country, hunting up the records of some local worthy for a literary friend, who had made the errand a pretext for helping her to a much-needed holiday. Her headquarters for the week had been an ancient and singularly quiet inn, in whose tiny parlour she had spent solitary evenings, save for the occasional eruption of a farmer or two with their wives, or a passing cyclist. On the last evening of all a stranded motorist had come, leaving his refractory car to the tender mercies of the neighbouring blacksmith, who thought he could "fix something to carry on with".

So he told her. She had been writing letters at the time, and had taken no notice of his entrance. But the landlady, bringing his sherry, had broken the ice by some chance remark, had drawn her in and left her involved in a conversation which had then developed as suddenly and deliberately as though the meeting had been planned. She was sucked into it, drawn under in a defenceless sort of condition, listening in amazement to an outpouring of personal history, countering it with fragments of her own: important fragments, flung down at random with a queer sense of detachment, as though this were an eddy in the stream of existence, a gap in which ordinary relationships were suspended and personal reticence had no place. And this was all the more strange because while the coin she tossed him was true, she knew that some of his rang counterfeit.

He was so happy nowadays, he assured her. All these difficulties there had been, at some time or another in his life, but he had weathered them all. Life as *they* had arranged it now was the ideal solution. *They* were agreed upon that. They agreed in everything. …

Why was he telling her all this, she had wondered. What was there at the back of this rush of words that was meant for her to hear? In the end he had asked for her address because, he said, he knew someone who might have more light to throw on the subject of her researches there. If he could discover anything of value he would send it on to her.

She had come back to her letters with a slight sense of disruption, such as one experiences standing on the platform of a railway station after an express has hurtled through, leaving a quivering air and a little twirling rubbish in its wake. But it had soon subsided. In the months that had followed she had lost all but a hazy impression of his person and a more distinct remembrance of a voice that ran up and down, excitedly, like a child's voice, but always with an undertone she could not seize.

Now he had written to give her the promised information—a couple of dates and a detail or two that might be of use to her friend.

"I'm so glad to have this excuse," he went on, "or I might never have had the courage to write at all. As it is, when you've read a little farther you'll tear my letter up, most likely, and that will be the end of it. Or perhaps you won't. I don't know what to think. Anyway, I'll risk it.

"Half of what I told you that day wasn't true, and I don't want to put the truth in this letter, because it wouldn't be fair. But I could *tell* you, and I believe you would listen, and if you would, just for once, I believe it would help me to see my way through all sorts of things more clearly. Now it happens that for two days next week I shall be absolutely and entirely alone here. The house is isolated; we have no neighbours; and if I fetched you from London in the car on Thursday and took you back on Friday, *no one would ever know.*"

It was here that she had broken off and laughed. The phrase was so unexpected, the underlining so melodramatic. At the second reading it infuriated her, and her fingers twitched to tear the letter in half. She was not used to doing things by stealth. But she read on, angry, incredulous, alarmed, and yet faintly pleased to find herself so remembered, so appealed to, and in such terms, trying to evoke some distincter image of the writer and recapturing only the voice, running up and down excitedly, as a child's voice does, and the rush of words that had left such a quivering silence behind.

The rest of the letter was explicit only as to the possibility of sitting by a log fire to thrash out all sorts of questions, and the reasons—some sort of presentiment apparently—for his belief that she could help him out. But common sense told her she could not leave it at that; and immediately two views of the situation began to fight for the mastery of her mind; commonplace adventure to be indignantly shunned, or vital experience in which she was already, as he seemed to suggest, to some extent involved.

"If I hear nothing by Wednesday," the letter concluded, "I shall know you have turned me down. But if you *will* come, just send me a line acknowledging the first part of this letter."

This gave her a respite, anyhow, and she decided to sleep on it. To-morrow, perhaps, the obvious decision would resolve itself out of the chaos of her present thoughts. Do what she would, however, through the great part of the night the two aspects of the affair kept running alternately across her mind with the weaving rhythm of a shuttle, and under the weaving lay a warp of fear she could not blink; the man might be mad.

In the morning, with the aptness of a sign from heaven, came a letter from a country friend announcing her visit to London on the following Thursday. "Do meet me for lunch," it said, "I shan't be up again for ages, and it's so long since we met."

Perversely enough, she felt exasperated, and consigned the friend to limbo on the spot. "What bad luck," she wrote, "I shall be away the best part of that week." She deliberately overstated it, so as to be left in peace, so as to give herself the chance of changing her mind up to the last minute. And then the folly, the absurdity of the whole thing rushed over her again, and lunch at her friend's club seemed the hand of Providence held out.

But she posted the letter and waited for her thoughts to settle. On the Sunday she visited some friends, and deliberately turned her mind to other things, with the result that by Tuesday evening she found herself disentangled from her cowardice and prepared to face all possibilities. The last few years had had a tinge of greyness about them, from which this adventure promised a strange, mad, momentary escape, something so incredible that she need render account of it to no one but herself. "And after all, life itself isn't so precious as all that nowadays," she reflected, a little bitterly, in conclusion.

But as she sat down to acknowledge his letter an idea occurred to her.

"Thank you so much for the particulars you give me," she wrote, "but there's just one point I'm not quite clear about. It's a shame to bother you any further, but could you tell me whether it was Langley senior or Langley junior who founded the local literary club?"

She laughed as she signed the letter. It reminded her of the game of "Secret Dispatches" she had invented with some cousin as a child.

But she achieved her object, for early the next evening the telephone bell rang and the "Wait a minute, please, … *You're* thrrrrough," prepared her for a trunk call.

"Is that Mrs. Norton?"

"Yes."

"I say, I've got your letter, but I'm not quite sure what it means. …"

The voice was faint at first, and she listened intently to catch the tone.

"… I mean, are you coming, or aren't you quite sure?"

It was louder now, and recognizable. More than that, it was normal, cheerful, sane.

"It means," she said, burning most of her boats, "that I'd like to come, but there are questions I want to ask you first. After all, we've only had an hour's conversation so far, and you've left me so much in the dark."

She heard a chuckle. "Yes, I know. I know it's rather absurd …"

"Well," she went on, "can you be here early enough for us to have half an hour's talk before we start off again? You've got a long way to come, haven't you?"

"The best part of eighty miles."

"As much as that? It's worse than I thought."

"But I can easily be with you by one, and we can start again at two—or does that sound too much like asking myself to lunch?"

"Come to lunch, of course, that will be much the best way."

"Don't bother about me, you know, a sandwich does for me. … So I may really come and talk it over?"

"Yes, you may."

"I say, that's awfully …" And here the operator cut them off.

She settled in her mind, before going to sleep, the questions she meant to ask him, the stipulations she intended to make. But the nightmarish sense of folly had vanished.

She slept late, and became aware on awakening of some peculiar quality in the light upon her ceiling. It seemed to have focused itself there, giving a sense of more than usual illumination at this wintry season. She glanced at the clock. Half-past eight. Why this Sabbath silence?

She sprang out of bed, and could not repress a cry of dismay. Sifting down past the window she saw a fine, dense, veil of snow. The whole world had turned a pale, ashen colour: furry blocks of wall and roof and chimney outlined dimly on a pinkish sky.

"He'll never come," she told herself, wondering how such a

transformation could have effected itself in so little time. The snow must have started overnight, to be lying so deep already.

The flat felt deathly cold, and she raked out and relighted the sitting-room fire before going to her bath.

She breakfasted by the fire, and then set to work to tidy the flat, expecting every moment to hear the telephone bell ring. But at eleven, since nothing had happened, she decided to go out and buy provisions. She would need lunch herself, even if he didn't come, she told herself; but at her return she set out a meal for two. Twelve o'clock passed, and at one the factory hooters blared out into the silence with teazing insistence. "There! That's the end of that!" they seemed to say.

But ten minutes later her door-bell rang, and she ran swiftly down the long flights of stairs like an automaton. She had the street door open before her mind had begun to work, and they greeted each other with an embarrassed smile.

"Come in. You must be frozen," she said, drawing him in out of the cold. Behind him, beside the kerb, stood a tiny car, laden with snow.

"I live at the top of the house," she explained, leading the way; and as she closed the door of the flat behind them she added, "When I saw the snow this morning I didn't think you would start."

"It's much worse in the country," he told her, "because it's drifted. But nothing would have stopped me." And he laughed. "Your clock's fast. I'm really only five minutes late."

"Do get warm by the fire while I heat the soup," she begged him; but he insisted on helping her. They drew the table near the fire and sat down. He gave her the details of his journey—of his early start, to be on the safe side.

It was curious how little she had remembered of his face. He reminded her now of someone known to her years ago almost in childhood. She would have to go back a long way, she felt, to read him aright.

They had coffee, turning their chairs to the fire; and as he helped himself to sugar he took the plunge. "Now tell me what it is that's bothering you," he said.

"The secrecy, of course," she answered, "I hate this hole and corner business."

"I know. So do I. But there was no other way, really. And I think in this case it's justified."

"Couldn't you have stayed in London? That would have been so much better," she suggested.

"No," he said. "It wouldn't mean the same to me. I want you to see the house. I want you to get to know me where I belong, so that you will understand, and so that our meeting will remain real to me afterwards, because of the things you've touched and looked at. And it's not only me you're going to help, remember. If I can see it all from the outside, it may make a difference to her too."

"Well, but tell me *about* your wife," said Elizabeth. "I don't understand. You said you were so happy."

"We used to be happy. I'm still very fond of her. But we're all at sixes and sevens now. I've lost a lot of money since the War—put a lot into cotton when it was booming, and lost every penny of it. She's sore about that, because her people were against it at the time. And other things aren't paying as they used to (everybody's in the same boat I suppose) so I can't help thinking the only way is to sell the estate, house and all, and go and live in some quiet little place."

Elizabeth made a gesture of assent, but he took her up.

"It'd be an awful wrench for me, you know. The place has been ours for generations."

"Of course … I know …"

"But there are big mortgages on it, and it doesn't seem much use. …"

"What does your wife say?"

"She wants to keep it for her boy. She was a widow when I married her, you know, with a boy of her own, and I've adopted him. She refused to have another child, though I'd have given anything to have a son of my own. Still, I'm almost as fond of this one as if he *were* my own. Only," he turned a rueful face to Elizabeth, calling her to witness the unreasonableness of women, "only, now she's jealous of his caring for me, so I'm never in the right."

"Is there any money coming to the boy, so that he can run the estate another day?" asked Elizabeth.

"Her people have some money, and I think that's what she's banking on. She's up there now, discussing things with them. But she doesn't realize what a lot of money a place like this runs away with, and how badly in debt we shall be by the time we come into any. Her people aren't shelling out now, that's very certain."

"What do you really want to do?"

"I don't know. That's just the point. I want to get away from a false situation, from all this pretence and keeping up appearance. We're only living in a corner of the house as it is, and I feel that we should be just as happy—much happier in fact—in a cottage somewhere, and all we saved would help to send the boy to college. … And then I funk it. I dread the wrench, and the way she'll take it—it might break up everything between us."

"But where do I come in?" asked Elizabeth, puzzled.

"You come in," he said, "because you're the only person I've ever met who belongs to both worlds. I mean, we began the same, but you've chucked all that, or it's chucked you, and you don't mind. You've knocked about, and settled down among people who don't care two hoots for money or position, probably, so long as they can get other things they want more. So you can see both sides. You know what there is to give up and what there is to gain. You can hold the balance fairly, because you've been through the struggle yourself and got outside it once for all. That's true, isn't it?"

"Yes, it's true," said Elizabeth.

"You know," he went on, "I really did have an extraordinary feeling when I walked into that pub. As though everything was happening twice as fast as usual. 'Come along, come along, it's waiting,' I felt. And when I saw you sitting there I knew just what was going to happen. I knew I'd only got to clear out the landlady and start off. I wasn't a bit afraid of you. Only when it came to talking about her I felt it wasn't fair somehow—not there, not just yet. And I puzzled and puzzled how to get hold of you again. I can hardly ever get away by myself, you know. … And then this opportunity came. You won't let it slip, will you?" he went on anxiously, "You *will* come?"

"Yes," she said, "if I can really help, and it's the only way. But in that case you must promise me that the secrecy is really foolproof."

He looked at her very hard.

"Oh, not for myself," she assured him. "I'm not afraid in that way. But it would be damnable to hurt someone else."

He drew a long breath of relief. "It's really all right," he said. "I've thought of everything. Absolutely everything. The woman who works for us by day is laid up and can't come for a week. The nearest village is three miles off and the nearest station seven."

"That sounds a little sinister," said Elizabeth, smiling. "Do you know, it's more than once crossed my mind that this adventure might be going to end in a hastily dug grave in a corner of your garden."

"You thought I might be cracked. I don't wonder. I've had qualms about you too," he admitted. "For all I knew, there might be someone in the background who would make it hot for me another day."

"I told you I had no ties," she said. "There's no one to come down on *you*." She burst out laughing. "What a crazy affair this is!" she cried. "Here are we planning a sort of elopement, and confessing we've been afraid of murder and blackmail."

"You aren't afraid now?" he asked her.

"No, not now."

"Nor am I. So let's be off. It's not going to be an easy drive."

"Right. I'll rake out the fire and put the guard on."

"No, let me do that. You don't *mind* the long drive? You won't be cold?"

"No, I shall enjoy it. I'll wrap up in everything I can find."

The car looked very tiny, a forlorn little hermit-crab's shell standing by the kerb. But they settled into it more comfortably than she had expected, and she felt a positively childish thrill at setting out into the unknown in anything so frail—it might have been an affair of chairs and string in the nursery. The street was empty, the houses were grey against the colourless sky, and all noises deadened by the heavy wadding of snow.

There was seldom much traffic in the side streets of this northern suburb, and the car, threading its way steadily towards the fringe, was soon out on a broad road leading northward into a part of the country Elizabeth had never seen. In her mind till then it had been a green patch on the map, low-lying, flat, intersected by little rivers, stretching for miles beside the central spine. But now the map was white, with wavering lines of hedge and copse finely engraved upon it. She caught herself guessing at the scale of it—two inches to the mile, perhaps—so dim and unreal it lay around her under the veil of drifting snow.

The little car held the road well, in spite of slithery expanses here and there on the surface, where other traffic had preceded them. Elizabeth glanced at her companion's hands, firm and sinewy on the wheel: easy concentration was in the set of his shoulders, the steadiness of his forward gaze.

"I'm a safe driver," he said, echoing her thoughts.

"I can see you are," she answered, "I trust you entirely."

"Good. I want you to trust me." And he smiled.

Decidedly there were long-past associations that were called up for her by the face she now saw in profile at her side. The rounded chin, the deep-set eye put her on the track of youthful adorations long outgrown. It was the type, so well-known to her then, whose instinct with animals is always flawless—the right gesture, the right tone, the right approach. But with human beings? There he might fail, she felt, as she looked at him, from having too few categories in which to range them. Good fellows and scoundrels, women who need protecting and women who don't—she suspected him of knowing no others, and that quite often he might be bewildered, caught at a disadvantage, by problems less simple than these would cover.

Into what category, for instance, was he putting her? Hardly among the helpless feminine, since it was on a belief that she had found, unaided, the solution he was seeking, that he was building. Yet that belief, she felt, was a little disturbing to him: a woman so self-reliant might be dangerous. The tension of his thoughts, which she suspected, seemed communicating itself to her by a sort of physical radiation. She found she was gripping the sill of the window beside her, holding herself rigidly aloof. She relaxed, let her shoulder rest naturally against his, and felt the strain slacken for them both. By and by he spoke.

As he elaborated his problem she saw increasingly that she had guessed aright in the main. His wife, of necessity, was a being to protect. His obligation in the matter was all the greater, it appeared, that he had persuaded her to marry him in preference to a richer man, whose affairs, unlike his own, had prospered since the War. He did not seem to think of her as a person capable of exercising free will. All she was doing now, without consulting him, was brought about by the influence of "her people". Yet the more he told of her, the more his wife emerged as a self-reliant, calculating, if not perhaps very well-advised individual. Elizabeth could only listen, questioning softly here and there, fearing as yet to disagree; and after a time he fell silent again.

His face now was a silhouette against the window. The headlights of the car threw two white shafts into space, and the windscreen wiper clicked steadily back and forth, clearing the fine dust of snow from the glass as it drove and drove against it ceaselessly. The world seemed dissolving under the gentle, insistent action of the snow, that was seen to be twisting in slow spirals across the light.

Suddenly he pulled up. "Now we're blocked," he said, lowering the window and peering out. Shouts were heard, and lights moved in the dusk ahead.

"What is it?" asked Elizabeth.

"I don't know. I'd better go and see." And he left her in the car and went away to reconnoitre.

"There's a lorry stuck in a drift," he said, when he came back, "jammed up with a wagon. Right across the road."

Elizabeth laughed. In this disintegrating world nothing was real enough to matter.

"There are three cars held up in front of us," he went on, "and some more coming along behind."

"What are you going to do?"

"D'you mind getting out and going a little way ahead? I don't want to upset you in the snow."

She got out obediently, and walked past the waiting line of cars. They had drawn in a little towards the middle of the road, but the space between the wagon and the bank looked very small. She passed it and looked back, waving her hand. The little car started, accompanied by shouts, and drove unswervingly down the narrow passage, missing the wagon by an inch.

"They said I couldn't do it," he said gleefully, as he helped her in, "and not one of the others will dare."

"Only a Cinderella's coach like this could get through," she teazed him.

"Now, don't you abuse my car."

The adventure had shaken them out of their serious mood. They discovered that they were hungry, and pulled up in the next town they came to for a heterogeneous meal. The inns looked gloomy and forbidding, but a teashop supplied them with food of sorts, and hot drinks, and a blazing fire that they were loth to leave.

For the rest of the journey the road was a white tunnel progressively bored out of blackness, and Elizabeth sat bemused, as though the windscreen wiper and the whirling snow were making hypnotic passes before her eyes.

A sudden change of direction aroused her. She was aware of stone gate-posts and snow-laden shrubs, and then with another swift turn the journey ended: the car was stationary beside a low-built door.

"We always come in the back way nowadays," he explained, "it saves such a lot of trouble."

He drew the key from its hiding place under the scraper and let her in, flashing an electric torch to show her the way.

"How warm it feels!" she said, appreciatively, standing, a little dazed still, in the long white passage that led away, as the road had done, into darkness.

"That's the boiler," he told her. "I stoked it up to bursting this morning before I left."

He pushed open a baize-covered door and led her up a narrow, uncarpeted staircase to the next floor. The passage they emerged upon seemed cavernous about the waving light of the torch, but at the opening of another door a soft glow of firelight welcomed her. The remains of a huge pile of logs and coal lay smouldering in an open fireplace, and blazed up at a touch as he raked them together.

"That's more cheerful," he said. "Do you mind sitting here for a moment while I get a light?"

When he had gone she looked about her at the room, as it revealed itself here and there in the light of the darting flames.

It was strange, of course, and yet familiar in its essentials: the glistening chintzes, the little tables, the fashionable weeklies scattered on the chairs.

He came in again, carrying a lamp. "We used to make our own electricity," he said apologetically, "but it was too expensive, so we've gone back to this."

Now the illusion was complete. With the smell of the wood fire and the scent—surely—of dried rose-leaves somewhere about the room—mingling with this faint but inescapable tang of paraffin, she was back in the story of her youth, about to turn the unread page that she had somehow missed.

"May I show you over the house?" he asked her, "or are you too tired?"

"Tired? Not a bit. I'd love to see it, of course."

He led her first to a room across a passage that was softly lighted by a little lamp and by a leaping fire. The flames threw the shadows of the bedposts towards her over the counterpane, and lighted the memory of nights in just such a bed, fevered with the pangs of youthful unrequited love. For of course she had been in love with all those young creatures of the past, with their glamour and dashing gaiety, and the traditional chivalry that had made them behave kindly to her in spite of themselves.

They had found her dull, unattractive, a little odd. She had seen their eyes light up for other women, and heard their voices quiver on a new note. She had danced with them, trying to be unaware, in the happiness of having their arms about her, how their glances followed others round the ball-room.

"This is my room," said her guide. "I've tried to make it comfortable for you."

She praised the fire, already in such a glow. "How did you manage it?"

"I laid it very carefully," he told her, "and rushed in to light it just now. I didn't want your room to look cold and strange."

"You must be a magician," said Elizabeth. The room welcomed her. It acknowledged her right to be there.

"But now you'll want your coat again." He had it on his arm, and helped her into it. "The rest of the house will be horribly cold."

He took a hurricane lamp from a table in the passage, and led her down to a swing door that shut off this little inhabited corner of the house. As it swung to, softly, behind them, she had a strange sense of having gone still farther back in time.

He took her first into the library, a great long room with lofty, shuttered windows, and bookcases reaching to the ceiling. As he swung the lantern up, she saw that these were for the most part empty. In the lower shelves a few folios leant forlornly against each other here and there; along the shallow topmost ones ran an assortment of little calf-bound volumes, incomplete sets of the *Spectator*, the *Rambler*, the *Monthly Magazine*, that the dealers had scorned when they cleared the rest away.

"The books were all sold in my father's time," he said. "That's his portrait over the mantelpiece."

He shifted the lantern, and the features defined themselves amid the blur of the glazing on the paint. The same eyes. The same chin.

A portrait filled the space above the door at either end of the room, taking the story of the race back two generations, telling it with the same features, the same air of romanticism, of obstinate quixotry. The faces, glowing sombrely amid the brilliance of the uniforms, were all the more alive in the lofty, shrouded room, for the emptiness of the shelves, that made Elizabeth think of rifled tombs.

Their steps sounded hollowly on the polished boards as they made their way to the farther door.

It gave on a broad landing from which the two arms of a wide staircase swept down to the entrance-hall. On one of these their footfalls were now muted entirely by a deep carpet; and the lantern, flashing regularly from portrait to portrait as they moved downwards, showed the race receding steadily farther into the past. Above the suits of armour in the hall hung the portraits of those who had worn them, and the light, calling out the gleams of real and pictured steel, translated them to Elizabeth's inner ear to faint, metallic clashings.

They threaded a sequence of ceremonial rooms, with tall windows shuttered, chandeliers veiled, and furniture of several periods standing meaningly grouped, like actors awaiting the rise of a curtain, who had meanwhile fallen asleep.

Their journey brought them back to the hall, and for a moment they paused, caught by the hush within and the hush without. On the steps beyond the great entrance door they could feel the cold pressure of the mounting snow, its muffling carpet that evened the steps, merging the lowest with the paving of the court, the court itself with the roadway and the wide, flat park, the park with the limitless world. They had come to the outskirts of time, and only a door barred them from eternity.

Elizabeth shivered. He led her up the other arm of the staircase, beneath the portraits of the women who had inspired the dreams and swayed the lives of the men facing them across the way. No two of them were alike, save in their air of complete detachment, of utter unconcern for the beings that gazed on them from the opposite wall. Fresh from the hands of would-be Vandycks and Lelys, they had an inward gaze of concentration or a mocking stare that made them impervious to the dreams, the devotions, the silent, impassioned appeal that still flowed towards them across the dim gulf of time.

From the landing they turned this time into a corridor, and at the end of that into a room where Elizabeth felt her breath catch sharply, as though a presence, disturbed and put to flight, had glanced back at her from the farther door: her own ghost, or his, she could not have said which. The tall fender, the rocking-chair, the framed "coloured supplements" with their bye-gone sentimentality, had brought her with a jolt into a past that was still emotionally near.

In a corner stood a rocking-horse, with nostrils distended and eyes agleam, staring bravely into space.

"I used to ride that horse for hours at a time," he said, "making up all sorts of adventures for myself."

"I had a rocking-horse too," said Elizabeth.

She leaned against the door-frame, taking it all in. The pilgrimage of the mind begun here in firelit security, the arduous journey; and the crumbling of dreams in the light of day. She felt knit to him suddenly in a strange solidarity, as though she could barely disentangle her identity from his.

A sigh, hers or his, broke the spell. He closed the door, and they made their way back to the sitting-room, where the tang of paraffin and the crumbling rose-leaves hung heavier than before in the warmth of the fire.

For a moment they sat in silence. Then he laughed. "Now that I've got you here, I'm shy of you," he told her.

"I'm shy too," said Elizabeth. "It's absurd. But I know what it is. You've been planning the whole thing beforehand—what you would say, and what I would answer—and now we've both got stage fright. Come here. ..." She patted the sofa on which she was sitting. "I'm real. You can put your arm round me, and say the first thing that comes into your head."

"That's better," he conceded, as they leaned back among the cushions, her head on his breast.

"Now we can talk," said Elizabeth. "Tell me all about yourself from the beginning."

But it was not so simple. He zigzagged, as a snipe does at the outset of its flight. He related this incident and that, threw the torch-gleams on a lonely childhood merging swiftly into adolescence, upon the War, that had followed as swiftly, and from which he seemed to have emerged less shaken than many: putting the memory of it behind him as of a traditional duty traditionally accomplished. *There* was not the rub.

A log fell away from the burning pile on the hearth, and shot a stream of embers in their direction. He rose, replaced the log, and swept the embers back with an absorbed expression. He took a turn about the room.

Elizabeth felt a break of some kind impending. The thread spinning between them was wearing thin. She sat quiet, letting all he had told her so far coalesce into an image of him, with which to maintain contact.

Once more, half consciously, she slackened her pose, as though to relax a physical tension, and her gaze shifted from the fire to a little bookcase on the wall by her side. The light played on the titles. Prose and verse, they ranged through several centuries: in the romantic tradition every one. The lettering on one was blurred. She could not decipher it, and put out her hand instinctively to take the book from the shelf. The movement recalled him to her.

"Those are most of the books I read," he said. "Some of them were my father's, and I've added to them by degrees."

He sat down by her again, and they resumed, as though by tacit consent, the same position as before. But this time he took her hand in his, as though to establish a closer communion.

He plunged into the story of his marriage: a quixotic marriage founded, as she had earlier half-guessed, upon a dreaming misconception of the nature of women.

He had shown her no picture of his wife, but through his unconscious revelation of mistakes that had thrust them apart, she saw a woman's face hardening into the detachment, the self-refusal of all the portraits on the stair-case.

"But why must you always do everything for her? Why not treat her as an equal, share your mind with her, let her act *with* you?" she burst out at last.

"Because I don't want to," he confessed. "I want to be the one to make sacrifices. I love to think she's weak, and that I'm strong."

"How appallingly selfish," said Elizabeth.

"I know. I know that quite well," he conceded. "It's one of the bad things about me. And there are others ..."

He talked rapidly now, at random, pausing now and then to say "You don't *mind* my telling you these things? I've never talked like this to anyone before."

"Of course I don't mind," said Elizabeth. "It's what I'm here for, isn't it?"

What she was there for defined itself more and more clearly in her mind as he went on. She had once watched the emancipation of a dragon-fly from an earlier stage of existence, as it clung to a reed above the level of the water from which it had emerged, and dragged itself from the outworn shell of its earlier self. Here, she could see it now, an escape of the same kind was to be attempted. Not simply from the house, as he had at first suggested, with the responsibilities it entailed, but from the self that had been formed by its traditions. A self that now seemed to him subaqueous, unfulfilled, out of touch with the realities of earth and air and sun.

At their chance encounter at the inn he had seen her as something that had escaped into freer air, and romantically, in some far more romantic parable, no doubt, than the one she had hit upon, he had staged in this planned re-counter the setting for a miracle. She was the reed.

A broken reed, mused Elizabeth sadly, as she listened, for she had no faith in miracles. She could not make over to him, simply, what greater freedom she had won for herself.

She listened intently as he tried to define himself, to see himself for the first time, as it were, detached from his native element and ready for escape. It would not do. He was still thinking in terms of his old existence, in the pattern handed down to him from the portraits on the stairs. Something deep within him condemned him to be the last of his race, rather than, as he had dimly imagined himself, the first of a new generation.

She felt a pang of unreasoning remorse, as though in all these years she ought to have been aware of him, aware that he was prisoned, left behind.

"Why don't you read," she cried, reasoning with him, "other sorts of books; get into touch with different people? Our old world is crumbling, as you say, but there's a new one in the making for us to possess."

"It's *too* new. I can't face it," he said. "Not alone."

"One has to face most things alone," said Elizabeth, "but it's worth it."

He was silent. Leaning forward he stared into the embers, where a last little flame at that moment flickered and died out.

"If I had you ..." he began.

"Surely we can be friends," said Elizabeth. "We can write. I can introduce you to people ..."

He shook his head. "It wouldn't do. There's no place for you, even as a friend, in her scheme of things. She wouldn't understand ... There's only to-night ... To-night is mine ..."

"To-night is mine," thought Elizabeth, with a sudden rush of happiness, though at the same instant she knew the happiness for what it was—a shred of an unlived past, to be lost as soon as recovered. The tenderness, kindling to passion, that she felt for the man beside her, belonged to a meeting that might have happened, but did not, years ago.

A little clock somewhere in the room chimed a late hour. The embers on the hearth fell apart, turned rapidly grey, and Elizabeth stared at them as though by the intentness of her look she could keep them alive.

"You don't like me a bit," he said in a changed, harsh voice.

"But I *do*."

"Really? Do you mean that?" he whispered, dragging her close, looking deep into her eyes.

Waking next morning they lay for a time in the candle-glow that tinged the bedposts and the patterned canopy above them, talking softly. They might have been friends and lovers for a lifetime, the tenderness and passion of the night merging in one their past, separate existences. They talked in low, contented voices, bartering confidences at random, building up a fragile world that should enclose them; and within the radius of the candle-light time for a little while stood still. But at the window a thin blade of daylight edged in under the blind, creeping towards them, bringing a different day.

Elizabeth was dressing when a double knock resounded at the back door, and for a moment, to her confusion, she was swept by a sense of guilt. It faded, but the spell was broken.

"The post has come," he told her, when he had called her in to breakfast. "The poor old chap could hardly get here for the snow." His voice had a tinge of anxiety. "It will be worse than yesterday, doing the two journeys in the time. I've got to be back here to meet the seven o'clock train."

"Put *me* into a train at the nearest station," said Elizabeth. "That would save all the trouble."

He shook his head. "No. I brought you down and I'm taking you back. But we shall have to hurry."

They had risen early. In a short time they had put the place in order, banking up the fires as yesterday. But on the mantelpiece in the sitting-room two letters stood waiting. "Mrs Staffield. Mrs Staffield." The whole room stood waiting. It had an alien, unfriendly look.

He brought the car round to the door.

"The snow has covered all our tracks of yesterday," he said.

"It will soon have covered to-day's," said Elizabeth, watching the snow sift into her latest footprint.

The body of the house was invisible from where she stood, masked by a shrubbery planned to conceal the kitchen entrance. But from the angle of the drive she saw the steps mounting under the snow to the great porch, like a wave against a cliff. Then the trees of the gateway shut everything out; and with a shock of sadness she felt her youth fade from her a second time, more definitely and irreparably than it had done by the slow passing of ordinary years.

A long level road lay before them, with obliterated hedges, under a leaden sky and the persistent, dizzying, sifting veil of snow.

The conversation lagged. Having no plans, they had too much and yet too little to talk about. The play was over; the curtain should have been rung down. The weight of the hours in front of her drove at Elizabeth's breast with the weight of years, as though in this interval before taking up her life again she must re-live all the years from her youth till now. She must re-endure the crash, the plunge into the world unripe, unready; the blundering search for some foothold, some steadying purpose; and then her late marriage and early widowhood, and the blanker loneliness that had ensued. It all pressed against her with a physical pain, as though the walls of a tunnel were falling in upon her. And at the end of the tunnel there was nothing. Her friends, her work seemed nothing now beside the happiness of a few hours since, that was fading in her hands like a dying ember. She watched it fade. She could have blown it into life again, perhaps, by showing him her thoughts, appealing to his pity. Piteousness, the romantic aspect of it, would have been her trump card. But she tossed it aside. Pity, she saw, should rather be for him, since she had not helped him, since, in the stream that was tearing them apart again, she would keep her head above water and he perhaps would drown.

He sat beside her at the wheel, brooding, and suddenly exclaimed "It's too bad. Your fire will be out. The place will be wretchedly cold. I shall hate to leave you like that."

"Oh, that's all right," said Elizabeth cheerfully. "I'm so used to it. I shall have a good fire going in no time."

She made herself numb to the pressure of the pain, freed herself enough to start a discussion. But their minds were not in tune; they were soon on the verge of a quarrel, and she had to laugh it off. She turned the subject, felt silence growing on them again, and resigned herself to it and to the blankness ahead.

The tentacles of London came straggling out through the snow, the houses standing up in rows like the suckers of an octopus. Far away at the centre was a dingy mass. Through the tortuous by-ways they came to Elizabeth's street, empty and blanketed with snow.

The staircase had a cavernous, damp smell, that seemed to have crept into the flat.

As they embraced in the dusk of the little hall, "Perhaps we shall meet again after all," he said, but neither of them believed it.

She heard his footsteps dwindling down the long stair-case, and the tremor of the house ran through her with the closing of the street door. Then, faint and final, the car door slammed, and the motor, with a little gasp, like a creature wakened from a dream, churred softly away into the silence.

NOVEMBER FAIR

FFAIR GAEAF

KATE ROBERTS

Translated from Welsh by Joseph P. Clancy

There they were, a train compartmentful, with their faces towards November Fair—what was left of it. It was fate threw them all together there like this, until it made them like one family, with each one having his own pleasure in looking forward to November Fair.

In one corner sat Esra (there is no need to give his surname, since nobody used it), wearing a black bowler that tapered to the front and to the back, and a topcoat that had once been black with the border of its velvet collar curling a bit. He was a tall, thin man, with eyes almost too small for you to be able to tell their colour. This was the first time he would be in the Town for a year. He was a farmhand. You couldn't tell what his age was. He could be fifty-five, and he could be thirty-eight.

Beside him sat Gruffydd Wmffras and his wife Lydia—two people about sixty years old, but he was looking better than she was. There was a healthy look on him—his skin weather-coloured and his cheeks red. He'd show two good rows of his own teeth in laughing. He too was wearing a black bowler, a bit newer than Esra's, and a thick black topcoat with a white hair on it. His wife was thin, and had lost many of her teeth without getting them replaced. The dints where her molars had been made her look old. She was wearing a black coat that was in its fourth winter now, and a new black hat that she'd got this year. But the hat didn't look fashionable, because the stack of her hair raised it off her head. Around her neck was a scarf of white lace fastened in front with a brooch.

In the other corner sat Meri Olwen, a neat, handsome girl, about twenty-five years old, wearing a new suit that she'd got at the end of the season. A blue coat and hat, grey silk stockings, and black morocco shoes.

Opposite her on the other seat sat Ben Rhisiart and his wife Linor—a young couple, just married. They'd been courting when they went to November Fair last year. He was a young farmer, farming a farm that his father left him, and his mother was living with him and his wife. His wife and himself were wearing bright, cheap clothing—he wore a cap that came low on his head. She was fair-skinned but toothy, a fact that made her mouth look as though it belonged to someone with a great idea of herself.

Between them and the other door sat Sam, a six-year-old boy, and grandson of Gruffydd and Lydia Wmffras, getting to go to the fair with his grandfather and grandmother for the first time. But already, on his way to the station, he'd attached himself to John, who at this moment was whistling a folk song in the vestibule. John was a thirteen-year-old boy allowed to go to the fair on his own. He was long accustomed to going everywhere on his own, or for the most part, with someone's animals. But today, no one was taking an animal to the fair, so he could go there in the afternoon just like everyone else. He didn't much care to have Sam trailing after him, but still, Sam's grandmother had given him sixpence on the way to the station, and the hint was enough for John.

The inside of the compartment was warm, the two windows were shut to the top, and the steam from the passengers' breath was shrouding the windows. Outside for miles was a bare countryside of farms—the fields perfectly bare, and the houses looking lonely and unsheltered on the hillsides, and from the train like this looking uninteresting to those who didn't live in them. It was nice in the warm train, with the mist on the windows half concealing the greyness of their daily life on the farms. Only John bothered to rub the window, because the only charm of going in a train to him was being able to look out. Inside, everyone was talking about everything, and Sam got more notice than anyone else because he could recite the name of every station to the Town in the proper order. He got pennies from the other passengers for being so knowledgeable.

After reaching the Town, everyone separated. Lydia Wmffras was very eager to have a talk with her sister, whom she hadn't seen for months, and so she asked John whether Sam could go with him. In a weak moment, she'd promised Sam that he could come with her to the Town for November Fair, and by now she'd regretted it, because her sole purpose in coming to town was to be able to see her sister Elin, who was living too far away for her to see her often.

As for Gruffydd Wrnffras, he was coming to the fair to look around and see who he could see. In the time gone by he'd come with cattle in the morning, though he sometimes would have only a barren cow and a calf or two. But now it wasn't worth coming such a distance. No one would ask what a cow was good for at a fair. But he needed to be able to come to the Town, and he began to ramble through the Square. There were plenty of people there, and plenty of motors with their noses all pointed the same way like a lot of greyhounds ready to start a race. He felt fine in being in the midst of plenty of people, and he wanted to talk to everyone. After dawdling and having a word with this man and that, he saw at last the one that he most wanted to see—Huw Robaits.

"Did you catch the fair this morning?" Gruffydd asked.

"Catch what?"

"Catch the fair?"

"You can't possibly catch something if it isn't there."

"There wasn't any fair, then?"

"There wasn't one animal here on this Square today. Do you smell the scent of a horse or a cow here? Not a chance! You have to go to Tom Morgan's sale to see a cow these days."

Gruffydd was surprised.

"I don't know what the world is coming to, indeed," the latter said. "Well, we'll all go to the Workhouse together, that's a comfort," Huw said.

"Have you begun slaughtering some of your animals?"

"No, not yet. Have you?"

"Yes; I slaughtered two lambs last week, but I won't slaughter any again. The butchers are raising too much of a row."

"You'll come for a pint to cheer up, old boy?"

And they went to a quiet tavern in Tre'r Go.

Elin, Lydia's sister, was waiting for her by the motor. Neither one of them had written to the other to say whether they would be in town or not. Each took it for granted that the other would be there.

"Your train was late," Elin said first thing.

"No, indeed; your motor was early. How are you, tell me?"

"Oh, all right I suppose, considering how poor a world it is. I want to buy a hat. Will you come with me?"

"Yes," Lydia said, with her heart in her boots, because she knew what sort of afternoon she would have with Elin.

"We'll go to the Golden Ewe," the latter said, "there are more hats there to suit someone like me. Tell me, are you getting much of a price for your milk?"

"Sixpence a quart; the same as the summer."

"You're lucky. A groat, that's what we're getting over there."

"How's that?"

"Some foreign old things came there and started selling it for a groat. It isn't worth your taking a horse out of the stable to set out with it."

Within a quarter of an hour Lydia and Elin were in the middle of a sea of hats in "The Golden Ewe".

"That one suits you splendidly, Mrs. Jones," the shop girl said about every hat that Elin tried on, with Lydia on the other side making faces and shaking her head to show that she didn't agree.

After she'd tried about fifteen, there was a somewhat frustrated look on Elin, so that it made you feel sorry for her.

"I don't know who'd ever buy a hat," Elin said. "They're making hats now for some old girls with bold faces, and not thinking of anyone who's beginning to get on in years."

"That's quite a pretty one," Lydia said. "That looks very good on you"—though it didn't look much better than the one before.

"You think so? Look, Miss, don't you have anything like the one my sister has? Where do you get your hats, tell me, Lydia? You have the prettiest hat on."

"You wouldn't need to cut your hair." And the two of them were close to quarrelling. At last Elin found a hat to please her for fifteen and eleven. And Lydia criticized her sister on the quiet for paying so much. Six and eleven her own had cost.

"Oh dear," Lydia said, after leaving the shop, yawning, "I need a cup of tea. Will you come and have it now, Elin?"

"Yes. We'll go to Jane Elis' restaurant in Pen Deits."

And there they went. It was beginning to grow dark by now. The dining-room of the restaurant was perfectly empty. A sluggish fire was burning in the grate. There were clean white cloths on every table, and the pepper-and-salt holder was shining even though it was yellow.

"How are you today, each of you?" Miss Elis said. "A heavy old day, isn't it? Have you been at the fair? If you can call that a fair. November Fair isn't what it was long ago. What would you like? Will you have a bit of hot beef with tea?"

"What do you say, Lyd?"

"Yes; hot beef with gravy would be quite nice."

"I wouldn't give a thank-you for a tea with some old cakes," Elin said. "Tell me, have you heard how Bob's wife Lora is?" (Bob was their brother.)

"I had a letter the day before, saying that she has terrible complaints. Bob's forever the one milking and doing everything outside."

"Bob had the luck of the draw when he had Lora."

They'd finished putting them in their places before Gruffydd and Huw Robaits arrived there.

"Who wants to treat me to tea?" Huw Robaits said playfully.

"Yes," Elin said, "it wouldn't be much for you to treat us all, Huw Robaits. I never get a dram or anything from anyone now."

"Here's someone will treat you, Elin," Gruffydd Wmffras said, on seeing Esra putting his head past the door. "It's the old bachelors have money now."

And the five of them drank tea and ate hot meat and gravy for a long while.

Before going to the restaurant Esra had been walking the streets of the Town aimlessly. That was what he did every November Fair Saturday. He was a man too lacking in conversation to talk to much of anyone. He had neither friends nor sweetheart. Had it been possible to win the latter without talking, he would have tried to win the woman he saw in the Town every November Fair. He didn't rightly know who she was. He had a notion that she was in service somewhere. But once he had ventured to strike up a conversation with her, and it was always the same after that.

"How are you today?"

"Very well, thanks."

"It's a nasty old day, isn't it?"

"Yes."

"Have you been at the fair?"

"No."

"There isn't much of anything at all to see there."

"There isn't, is there? Well, I must go."

And Esra would never have enough heart to ask her to come

and have tea with him or for a walk. He'd seen her again this year, and the conversation had been the same. But Esra hadn't gained enough strength to ask her. By the time he reached the restaurant he was quite glad that he wouldn't have to pay for anyone's tea but his own. He had a bit of a fright when Gruffydd Wmffras suggested playfully that he treat them all to tea. He was one of those people who are too tight-fisted to enjoy frivolous talk about money.

After leaving the station Meri Olwen walked straight to Huw Wmffras' old shop, where she was to meet her sweetheart, Tomos Huw. He was a quarryman, living eight miles from the place where she was a maidservant. Meri Olwen preferred that Tomos Huw live as far from her as that, because she had ideals. And one of those ideals was that you had better not see your sweetheart too often—as one would if he were living in the same village. She was a good girl for any mistress. She would work unmercifully between every two turns of courting so that the time would go by swiftly, and because she knew that she'd be sure to enjoy herself when a courtship evening came. It was only work could make her forget her yearning to see Tomos. And yet, she was certain in her mind, should she see Tomos often, this yearning would lessen, and so she would have less pleasure when she was in his company.

All the way on the train she was scarcely able to conceal her craving to see Tomos, and when she walked over the Bont Bridd, she was feeling almost ill for fear that Tomos wouldn't be there.

Yes, he was there, talking and fooling with three girls, with the girls laughing at the top of their voices and drawing everybody's attention to them. Meri Olwen stood still. Something cold went over her. Tomos was enjoying himself enormously. He was trying to steal a card that was in the hand of one of the girls, and she was refusing to give it to him. He was able to catch a glimpse of it at last, but not without the girl tugging at it many times. Tomos laughed loud and long after seeing what was on the card, and as he gave it back to the girl his eyes fell on Meri Olwen, and his face settled down. He left the girls unceremoniously, and came to Meri.

"Hullo, Meri, how are things? Your train was early, wasn't it?"

"No earlier than usual."

"Where shall we go?"

"I don't care in the least where."

"Come for tea now?"

"No, I prefer to have it later."

"We'll go for a stroll to the Quay then."

Meri Olwen's heart was like a piece of ice, and her tongue had stuck to the roof of her mouth.

"You're very quiet today."

"There's need for someone to be quiet, since some can make so much of a row."

"Who's making a row now?"

"You and those girls just now."

"A person has to have a bit of a lark sometimes—if you'd seen the funny postcard someone had sent to Jini."

"I don't want to hear anything about it."

"Tut, you're much too solemn."

"Yes; mercifully, I could never fool with boys like that."

"Oh! jealousy, I see."

And Meri Olwen wasn't able to give him any answer, because he'd spoken the truth.

She went ahead, with him trailing after her.

"You'd better go back to your Jini, with her filthy jokes."

Tomos stood there, bewildered. He'd never heard Meri Olwen talk this way before. She was one of the mildest persons.

She walked on and on. She was pounding her heels heavily on the ground, and she found herself within an hour in a village she didn't know. There she began to feel cold. How much she'd looked forward to this day for a fortnight! It wasn't often she could afford to come to the Town. She'd looked forward not only to seeing Tomos, but also to having tea with him in Marshalls, and being able to show people like Ben and Linor, who had just married, that she too was on the way to doing that. But now her ideal was shattered. She walked back to the Town slowly, crestfallen. She didn't go anywhere to have tea. She went to the waiting room of the station to wait for the seven-o'clock train.

Ben Rhisiart rushed out of the station and ran directly to the football field. The Town was playing against Holyhead. He was to meet Linor in Marshalls by tea-time. Linor walked slowly along the street and looked at the window of every shop. She had a longing for every grand article of clothing she saw. She'd be on the brink of going in to buy a blouse or a scarf when she'd remember that she couldn't afford them. After reaching the druggist's shop she went straight in without a second thought, and bought face powder and a bottle of scent. She walked on slowly afterwards, expecting to see some of her old friends. She'd looked forward to seeing some of them today; not that she wanted to talk to them as old friends, but because she wanted to make their mouths water as a young married woman. But she saw none of them. She caught a glimpse of Tomos Huw running to catch one of the motors on the Square, with his face very red. But he didn't see her—and that was a pity, because she'd have been glad if he'd seen her.

Tired of walking around, she went into Marshalls to sit down and wait for Ben. She felt contented there. Could walk on carpet and look at nice food and flowers and plenty of people. How different from the food she usually had. Her pastry crust was never a success. It was tough as an old shoe. And how should one expect it to be otherwise with the oven broken? And not a chance of mending it while her mother-in-law kept saying it was fine; that it had baked very well for her that way for the last twenty years. Perhaps it did bake bread; but then, why would anyone go baking bread, with the bread wagon calling every day? But as for pastry crust, you couldn't buy that in the country. But today, anyway, she could have tiny pink and yellow pastries, crusts as if they'd been puffed up, with cream inside them. Oh, she was happy—except when she'd remember her mother-in-law. That was the only thorn. Her words today, before they set off, were grating in her ears. "I don't know what's got into you wanting to go to the fair, indeed, with times so bad. And another thing, there isn't any winter fair now, the way there was long ago. There's no home-made cheese, or seed-buns, or griddle-cakes, or anything like that, or anyone like the Bardd Crwst singing ballads." A nuisance, that's what her mother-in-law was, to tell the truth, always talking about "long ago" and spouting proverbs against the extravagance of this age. What if she knew that her daughter-in-law had face powder in her bag now? And what if she knew that Ben would be paying some four shillings for tea for two? Presently Ben came, and many others with him, until they almost filled the room. The atmosphere was warm, and the electric light was shining dazzlingly on the aluminium teapots.

Ben hadn't much enjoyed himself at the football field. The old fiery spirit that once existed between this town and Holyhead had died.

The two of them enjoyed their tea.

"What do we want to do now?"

"We may as well finish it off, and go to the pictures," Linor said.

"I'd thought to go home with the seven-o'clock train."

"Tut, come to the pictures. Perhaps we won't be down again for a long while."

And so it was agreed.

John wasn't very pleased that Sam's grandmother had attached the latter to him for the entire afternoon. John had his own ideas about spending a day at a fair. Half the fun was getting to be there on his own, without anyone to interfere with him, and being able to test his knowledge of geography where he was completely ignorant of it a few years ago. But now he had to look after Sam, and he was too little to be able to admire John's extensive knowledge of the streets of the Town. The two of them followed their noses until they reached the Square. There was nothing at all new there to John. The only difference between this and any other Saturday was that there was a pull-away stall, and it was for this he was aiming.

But Sam wanted to stand at the dish stall so he could see the man rap and fling the plates and yet not break them.

"I want to buy a plate to take home to mam," Sam said.

"You'd much better take her indian rock," John said; "she has plenty of plates." In spite of all his knowledge, John didn't rightly know how to bargain at a sale.

"Look," he said to Sam at the pull-away stall, "try aiming at the biggest piece there."

And Sam took a hot, sweaty penny from the middle of a fistful of pennies and gave it to the woman. Sam's tug was very weak, and the ball fell by a thin, slight piece of indian rock. John tried, and he got a thick piece. Sam insisted on trying again on seeing John's luck, but it was a thin one he got that time.

"Come away," John said, "or you'll spend all your money, and we have to get chips before going home."

They went to the Quay, and Sam was insisting on eating his indian rock that minute.

"Leave it, lad, or you won't have any to take home to your mother."

But Sam didn't listen.

"This is the best shop in town for chips," John said, after they arrived at a shop in —— Street.

He made Sam sit at a table there as if he were at home, and he took off his cap.

"What do you want?" said the waitress.

"Threepenny worth of chips for me, and two for him," John said.

"No; I want threepenny worth," Sam said, and began acting up.

"Oh, all right," John said. "Mind that you don't leave a single one."

Sam was groaning long before he finished his threepenny

worth, and he began to droop. In a little while something strange happened to John's eyes. He was looking at Sam, and he saw his face was green.

"What's the matter with you?" he said to Sam.

"Need to puke," he said.

And at the word there Sam was, throwing up.

"Oh! you bad-mannered little brats," the waitress said when she arrived.

"He couldn't help it, indeed," John said, with Sam crying his eyes out by now.

"Never mind; we'll go look for your grandmother," John said.

And they found her as she was coming out of the restaurant in Pen Deits.

John went off to enjoy the rest of his day as he wished, and you could have seen him after a while gazing at the rabbits and the birds in the market gallery of Llofft yr Hôl.

It was a quite worn-out little band that gathered together to meet the seven-o'clock train. Lydia and Gruffydd Wmffras were looking extremely happy; Meri Olwen miserable, and Sam pale and quiet. John was whistling by the book stall. Esra was an entirely different man. He'd had three pints after the pubs re-opened. This was his only luxury in a whole year. He came towards the others mumbling a song, with his hat tipped back and his face sweating.

"Hullo, old love; where's your sweetie this winter fair evening?" he said to Meri Olwen.

Esra grasped her head and turned it towards him. On seeing

Esra, the silent man, so talkative, and seeing the strange look on him, Meri Olwen began laughing uncontrollably.

"You have a sweetheart?" Esra said. At that the train came in. Everybody rushed for a place.

And in the rush Esra took hold of Meri Olwen, and pulled her into a compartment apart from the others.

In the moving-picture house, Ben and Linor were slouching together, totally lost in a picture that showed the night life of New York, beautiful women in expensive clothing imbibing drinks whose names Ben and Linor had never heard of, with affectionate men gazing deep into their eyes.

They didn't remember there was such a thing as a train.

MY LIFE WITH R. H. MACY

Shirley Jackson

And the first thing they did was segregate me. They segregated me from the only person in the place I had even a speaking acquaintance with; that was a girl I had met going down the hall who said to me: "Are you as scared as I am?" And when I said, "Yes," she said, "I'm in lingerie, what are you in?" and I thought for a while and then said, "Spun glass," which was as good an answer as I could think of, and she said, "Oh. Well, I'll meet you here in a sec." And she went away and was segregated and I never saw her again.

Then they kept calling my name and I kept trotting over to wherever they called it and they would say ("They" all this time being startlingly beautiful young women in tailored suits and with short-clipped hair), "Go with Miss Cooper, here. She'll tell you what to do." All the women I met my first day were named Miss Cooper. And Miss Cooper would say to me: "What are you in?" and I had learned by that time to say, "Books," and she would say, "Oh, well, then, you belong with Miss Cooper here," and then she would call "Miss Cooper?" and another young woman would come and the first one would say, "13-3138 here belongs with you," and Miss Cooper would say, "What is she in?" and Miss Cooper would answer, "Books," and I would go away and be segregated again.

Then they taught me. They finally got me segregated into a classroom, and I sat there for a while all by myself (that's how far segregated I was) and then a few other girls came in, all wearing tailored suits (I was wearing a red velvet afternoon frock) and we sat down and they taught us. They gave us each a big book with R. H. Macy written on it, and inside this book were pads of little sheets saying (from left to right): "Comp. keep for ref. cust. d.a. no. or c.t. no. salesbook no. salescheck no. clerk no. dept. date M." After M there was a long line for Mr. or Mrs. and the name, and then it began again with "No. item, class, at price, total." And down at the bottom was written ORIGINAL and then again, "Comp. keep for ref.", and "Paste yellow gift stamp here." I read all this very carefully. Pretty soon a Miss Cooper came, who talked for a little while on the advantages we had in working at Macy's, and she talked about the salesbooks, which it seems came apart into a sort of road map and carbons and things. I listened for a while, and when Miss Cooper wanted us to write on the little pieces of paper, I copied from the girl next to me. That was training.

Finally someone said we were going on the floor, and we descended from the sixteenth floor to the first. We were in groups of six by then, all following Miss Cooper doggedly and wearing little tags saying BOOK INFORMATION. I never did find out what that meant. Miss Cooper said I had to work on the special sale counter, and showed me a little book called *The Stage-Struck Seal,* which it seemed I would be selling. I had gotten about halfway through it before she came back to tell me I had to stay with my unit.

I enjoyed meeting the time clock, and spent a pleasant half-hour punching various cards standing around, and then someone came in and said I couldn't punch the clock with my hat on. So I had to leave, bowing timidly at the time clock and its prophet, and I went and found out my locker number, which was 1773, and my time-clock number, which was 712, and my cash-box number, which was 1336, and my cash-register number, which was 253, and my cash-register-drawer number, which was K, and my cash-register-drawer-key number, which was 872, and my department number, which was 13. I wrote all these numbers down. And that was my first day.

My second day was better. I was officially on the floor. I stood in a corner of a counter, with one hand possessively on *The Stage-Struck Seal,* waiting for customers. The counter head was named 13-2246, and she was very kind to me. She sent me to lunch three times, because she got me confused with 13-6454 and 13-3141. It was after lunch that a customer came. She came over and took one of my stage-struck seals, and said "How much is this?" I opened my mouth and the customer said "I have a D. A. and I will have this sent to my aunt in Ohio. Part of that D. A. I will pay for with a book dividend of 32 cents, and the rest of course will be on my account. Is this book price-fixed?" That's as near as I can remember what she said. I smiled confidently, and said "Certainly; will you wait just one moment?" I found a little piece of paper in a drawer under the counter: it had "Duplicate Triplicate" printed across the front in big letters. I took down the customer's name and address, her aunt's name and address, and wrote carefully across the front of the duplicate triplicate "1 Stg. Strk. Sl." Then I smiled at the customer again and said carelessly: "That will be seventy-five cents." She said "But I have a D. A." I told her that all D. A.'s were suspended for the Christmas rush, and she gave me seventy-five cents, which I kept. Then I rang up a "No Sale" on the cash register and I tore up the duplicate triplicate because I didn't know what else to do with it.

Later on another customer came and said "Where would I find a copy of Ann Rutherford Gwynn's '*He Came Like Thunder*'?" and I said "In medical books, right across the way," but 13-2246 came and said "That's philosophy, isn't it?" and the customer said it was, and 13-2246 said "Right down this aisle, in dictionaries." The customer went away, and I said to 13-2246 that her guess was as good as mine, anyway, and she stared at me and explained that philosophy, social sciences and Bertrand Russell were all kept in dictionaries.

So far I haven't been back to Macy's for my third day, because that night when I started to leave the store, I fell down the stairs and tore my stockings and the doorman said that if I went to my department head Macy's would give me a new pair of stockings and I went back and I found Miss Cooper and she said, "Go to the adjuster on the seventh floor and give him this," and she handed me a little slip of pink paper and on the bottom of it was printed "Comp. keep for ref. cust. d.a. no. or c.t. no. salesbook no. salescheck no. clerk no. dept. date M." And after M, instead of a name, she had written 13-3138. I took the little pink slip and threw it away and went up to the fourth floor and bought myself a pair of stockings for $.69 and then I came down and went out the customers' entrance.

I wrote Macy's a long letter, and I signed it with all my numbers added together and divided by 11,700, which is the number of employees in Macy's. I wonder if they miss me.

THE COLD

Sylvia Townsend Warner

The Cold came into the household by Mrs. Ryder. At first she said she had picked it up at the Mothers' Union meeting; later—it was the kind of cold that gets worse with time—she attributed it to getting chilled through waiting in the village shop while that horrible Beryl Legg took over half an hour to decide whether she would spend her points on salmon or Spam. Never a thought for her child, of course, who by now should be getting prunes and cereals. Whoever the father might be, one would have expected the girl to show some maternal feeling—but no!

The next person to get The Cold was old Mr. Ryder, the Rector's father, and he immediately gave it to old Mrs. Ryder. They did not have it so badly, but at their age and after all they had gone through in London before they could make up their minds to evacuate themselves to their son's country parish, one had to put them to bed with trays, just to be on the safe side. Dry and skinny, they lay in the spare-room twin beds like two recumbent effigies on tombs, and chattered to each other in faded high-pitched voices. Segregated from the normal family life they had re-established that rather tiresome specialness which sometimes made it difficult to realise that they were really dear Gerald's parents. It is very nice to be cultivated, of course, but somehow in wartime it does jar to labour upstairs with a heavy supper-tray and hear, beyond the door, two animated voices discussing Savonarola; and then to hear the voices silenced, like mice when one throws a shoe in their direction, as one knocked on the door and called out brightly, "Supper, darlings!" and to know, as clearly as if one had seen it, that old Mrs. Ryder was stubbing out one of her cigarettes. That jarred, too, especially as she smoked such very heavy ones.

From the old Ryders The Cold descended to the third and fourth generation, to Geraldine and her two boys. Thence it leaped upon the Rector. "Leaped" was indeed the word. He had set out for the funeral looking the picture of health, he returned haggard and shivering, and so terribly depressed that she had said to herself: "Influenza!" But it was only The Cold—The Cold in its direst form.

"No!" exclaimed Mrs. Allingham, indefatigable secretary of the Women's Institute. "*Not* the Rector?"

"If you had been in church on Sunday you wouldn't need to ask."

For the indefatigable secretary was a matter for regret on Sundays, when she was more often seen taking her terriers over the Common than herself to Saint Botolph and All Angels. Such a pity!—for in every other way she was an excellent influence.

Recovering herself rather too easily, for it showed that such recoveries were nothing to the rebuked one, Mrs. Allingham went on: "All seven of you! For I can see you've got it too. You poor things! My dear, what do you do about handkerchiefs, now that the laundry only collects once a fortnight? Can I lend you some?"

"Stella washes them."

"Your marvellous Stella! What would you do without her? I hope she is still standing up."

"I can't imagine Stella failing us," said Mrs. Ryder with satisfaction.

In the sixth autumn of the war Mrs. Ryder was a little tired. She was feeling her age. Her last tailor-made was definitely not quite a success and, say what you will, people do judge one by appearances: she could not help noticing that strangers were not as respectful as they might be; though no doubt the unhelpfulness of Utility corsets played its part in the decline of manners. In the parish, too, there was much to grieve the Rector and the Rector's wife. The old, simple, natural order of things was upset by all these changes, the grocer's son actually a Captain, as much a Captain (and indeed senior in captaincy) as dear Geraldine's Neville, the butcher's wife in Persian lamb, the resolutions at the Parish Council only to be described as Communist, and the girls, her own Girls' Club girls, behaving so shockingly that she often wondered what the mothers of these poor American soldiers would think if they only knew what their sons were exposed to. But she had Stella. And having Stella she had all things.

No one could pick holes in Stella. There were no holes to pick. Stella was physically perfect, not deaf, nor halt, nor imbecile. Stella did not wear glasses and did wear a cap and apron. Stella was functionally perfect, she did not dawdle, she did not waste, she did not gossip, she was clean, punctual, reliable, she was always cheerful and willing, she scrubbed her own back kitchen and mended the choir surplices; and though of course her wages were perfectly adequate, no one could say that the Ryders bribed her to stay with them. Stella stayed through devotion, she could have got twice as much elsewhere. Finally, Stella was a good girl. In a time when manners and morality had gone down alike before expediency, when householders snatched at trousered and cigarette-smoking evacuees if the evacuee would "help with light domestic duties," when even the houses that ought to set an example employed girls with illegitimate babies and glossed over the capitulation with pretexts of being compassionate and broad-minded, Mrs. Ryder continued to boast the ownership of a virgin, a strong womanly virgin who wore skirts, fastened-up unwaved hair in a sensible knob, and said, "Yes, ma'am."

Naturally, one took care of such a treasure. Stella's cold was given quite as much consideration as any other family cold and dosed out of the same bottle. In the worst of the epidemic Mrs. Ryder said that if Stella did not feel better by midday she really must be sent to bed. For several evenings Mrs. Ryder and Geraldine washed up the supper dishes so that Stella might sit quietly by the stove with the surplices instead of shivering in the back-kitchen; and when Stella's cough persisted after the other coughs had died away Geraldine went in specially by bus to look for black-currant lozenges and came back with some wonderful pastilles flavoured with horehound.

But it was a long time before Stella's cough could be distinguished from the other coughs by outlasting them. The Cold was such a treacherous type of cold. When you thought you'd got rid of it, it came back. Like beggars, said old Mrs. Ryder (for they were downstairs again, one could not keep them in bed indefinitely). Like dandelions, said her son. Geraldine said that she believed it was nutritional. Of course one ought not to complain, the food was marvellous really, more marvellous than ever if one thought about poor old Europe; but still, it wasn't the same, was it?

She had met Mrs. Allingham, and Mrs. Allingham had enquired, of course, about The Cold, and had said that in 1918 everyone had just the same kind of cold, it was quite remarkable. What did the Grand-grands say? Did they have colds in 1918? "We had much better rum, and more of it," said old Mrs. Ryder. She looked at her husband very affectionately; he stroked his beard and looked back at her, and so they both avoided seeing Mrs. Ryder catch her breath like one who holds back a justified reproach because experience has shown that reproaches are vain. The Rector, even more imperceptive, remarked that it was very kind of his parents to make poor Stella a nightcap, he hoped it would do her good. He had seen rum do a lot of good when he was a chaplain in Flanders. Stella was a good girl, a very good girl. They would be badly off without her.

For some reason Mrs. Ryder and her daughter now began discussing how to-morrow they really must polish the stair-rods and the bathroom taps. They would make time for it somehow if Mrs. Ryder did the altar vases before breakfast and Stella took the boys with her when she went to the farm for milk. If the boys wore their rubber boots, the slush wouldn't do them any harm.

John was five, Michael was three. You couldn't really call them spoilt, they were just wartime, lacking the influence of a father about the house. But not spoilt. Besides, Geraldine liked boys to behave as boys; it would be too awful if they grew up like Neville's ghastly young brother who would sit for hours stroking the cat and turning off the wireless whenever it became worth listening to. A dressing-room had been made over as their play-room, but it was bleak up there, and naturally they preferred the kitchen. If anyone spoilt them it was Stella, who didn't seem able to say no to them.

And if they were rather fretful just now, it wasn't to be wondered at, it was The Cold.

The doctor's sister, a rather uncongenial character with independent means, used to refer to Mrs. Ryder and her daughter as Bright and Breezy. They had a great deal in common, she said, but Geraldine had more of it, and was Breezy. Geraldine now had more of The Cold. Her sneezes were louder, her breathing more impeded, her nose redder, and her handkerchiefs more saturated. Throughout The Cold Mrs. Ryder had kept on her feet: as a daughter-in-law, mother, grandmother, and wife to a Rector, she could not do otherwise; but Geraldine had not merely kept on her feet, she stamped and trampled. She scorned precautions, she went everywhere and kissed everybody, just as usual. She did not believe, not she! in cosseting a cold. What are colds? Everyone has them, they are part of English life. Foreigners have things with spots, the English have colds. She made having a cold seem part of the national tradition, like playing cricket and Standing Alone.

And so, when they had all got rid of The Cold and even Stella only coughed at night, Geraldine seemed to be breaking the Union Jack at the masthead when she woke the echoes of the kitchen with a violent sneeze, and asserted:

"I'm beginning another cold. And what's more, I can tell it's going to be a snorter. So watch out, one and all!"

"I do hope not, Miss Geraldine," answered Stella.

It was rather touching the way Stella still called her Miss Geraldine—as if to Stella the passage of time were nothing, a tide that flowed past the kitchen threshold but never wetted her feet.

"No jolly hope!"

Geraldine went out. Presently she could be heard telling her mother about the new cold. Mrs. Ryder sounded unenthusiastic; she said she only hoped it would not last so long this time, as otherwise it would spoil Christmas. Stella went on rubbing stale bread through a sieve for the wartime Christmas pudding. It needed a lot of breadcrumbs; in fact, you might as well call it bread-pudding and be done with it; but Mrs. Ryder said the children must be brought up to love Christmas. They stood on either side of the table, rolling bread-pills and throwing them at each other.

The recipe for the wartime Christmas pudding which needed a lot of breadcrumbs also called for grated carrot. When she had finished the breadcrumbs, and put them on a high shelf where she hoped the children might not get at them, Stella went into the back-kitchen and began to clean carrots over the sink. If you rub stale bread through a fine sieve for any length of time, you are apt to develop a pain between the shoulders. She had such a pain; and the change of climate from the kitchen which was hot, to the back-kitchen which was cold, made her more conscious of it. When she had cleaned the carrots she went back to the kitchen. The two little boys were still there and Mrs. Ryder had been added.

"Oh, Stella, I came in to say that I thought we would have onion soup to-night, as well as the fish-cakes. Mrs. Hartley thinks she has another cold coming on."

"Yes, ma'am. I wish to ..."

Mrs. Ryder swept on. "And, Stella, of course I know how busy you are, but all the same I think it would be better *not* to leave the babies alone in here. When I came in I found John playing with the flat-irons. Of course they were cold, but they might have been hot. Perhaps a little more thoughtfulness ... With such young children one cannot be too thoughtful."

"Very well, ma'am. But I wish to leave, ma'am."

"Beddy-bies, beddy-bies!" exclaimed Mrs. Ryder. "Come now, John, come, Michael! Kiss dear Stella goodnight, and off with you to your little beds. Now a nice kiss ..."

"Don't want to," said the child.

Mrs. Ryder seized a child under either arm, waved them in the direction of Stella's face, and conveyed them out of the room, shutting the door on them with a firm sweet, "God Bless you, my babies!" Then, flushed with exertion, with difficulty withstanding the impulse to go with them, she turned back, hoping that her ears had deceived her and knowing too well that they hadn't.

"I wish to leave, ma'am."

"Stella! What do you mean?"

"I wish to leave, ma'am."

There she stood, grating carrots as if the children's Christmas were nothing to her.

"But, Stella ... I *trusted* you. After all these years! Why, we all look on you as a friend. What has happened to you?"

Could it be, could it be? Stella was short and the kitchen table was high and anything may be happening behind an apron. In a convulsion of the imagination Mrs. Ryder rehearsed herself saying that one should not penalise a poor girl for a solitary slip, that kindness, a good home, the example of a Christian home-life which means so much, etc., etc. A harlot hope raised its head, and at the same moment she heard Stella say quite idiotically:

"I think I'm catching another cold."

"Good heavens, girl, is that a reason for going? I've never heard such nonsense."

"It's nothing but one cold after another—cold, cold, cold, work,

work, work! It's not a fit place for me. Both my aunties were chesty, and if I stay here I shall go the same way, I know it. What's more, I'm going to-morrow. I don't mind about my money, I'm going to-morrow. I want to get away while I've still got the strength to."

"In wartime," said Mrs. Ryder, in her sternest Mothers' Union manner, the manner only unfurled for urgent things like War Savings Rallies and Blood Transfusion Drives, "in wartime, when our boys are shedding their blood without a moment's hesitation ... and you are positively running away from a simple cold in the head. I cannot believe it."

Without a spark of incredulity she banged the door behind her.

There was the Rectory hall. There were the coats and the children's rubber boots and the umbrellas, and the brass letter-tray, and the copper gong, and the stair-rods ascending. There was Gerald writing in his study, and Geraldine gargling in the bathroom, and in the sitting-room the two old Ryders chattering like love-birds. Here was her home, her dear (except for the old Ryders), her dear, dear home, where everything spoke of love and loving labour: the happy, busy home that was—Mrs. Allingham's own words—a beacon to the parish.

But now ...

Not Stella? Not your marvellous Stella?

The words seemed to dart at her from every side, stabbing through the unsuccessful tailor-made into her ageing flesh. To-morrow the Sewing Circle met at the Rectory. Only self-respect withheld her from running back into the kitchen to throw herself on Stella's mercy, to beg, on her knees, even, to beg and implore that Stella would change her mind, would stay, would at any rate stay to see them over Christmas. Self-respect was rage and fury. Presently they died down. But she remained in the hall, knowing that any appeal to Stella would be in vain.

To-morrow the Sewing Circle met. They met at three in the afternoon. Stella would be out of the house before then. *She must be!* Mrs. Ryder thanked God that self-respect had stood like an angel between her and a fatal false step. "Stella has gone. Poor Stella! … I could not keep her." A few such words, and a grave grieved silence, nothing that was not true, strictly true; and the Sewing Circle might draw its own conclusions. Cooking, sweeping, scrubbing, doing everything that for so long Stella had done, she could still hold up her head.

THE PRISONER

Elizabeth Berridge

I

It was a frosty morning when the German prisoners first came to dig drainage ditches in the fields that lay beyond Miss Everton's garden walls. She was out with her dog in the chill air by the beech trees when two large lorries roared up past her across the grass and she had a glimpse of alien faces, of packed cardboard figures, cold and raw-looking. The rest of the valley was quiet, as if sheltered beneath a glass bell of cold and solitude. The hills stretched far beyond the fields and farms, the little trees—mostly bare—on their sides standing straight and close, like stitches on an old tapestry.

The trees that outlined the remains of a carriage drive across the fields to the lane beyond still kept their leaves, however, and each morning Miss Everton came to look at them. They seemed to her an echo of the past long and temperate summer, but somehow odd, like fruits out of season. They always shed their leaves late, but by November the gales had usually stripped them bare, it was nearly November now. Only the tough marigolds in the garden still went on producing their frostbitten suns; in the house a patch of brightness across a room, through a closed window, gave back summer's ghost.

The sun was coming up now, a long way off in the clear blue of the sky. But it warmed Miss Everton's hands, cold and clenched on the sticks she had gathered so that she could look away from the men as they jumped from the backs of the lorries. For some time they had been calling to each other in mirthless foreign voices, groaning with stiffness and cold, beating their hands together with a sound that carried in the petrified air.

A rustle disturbed her, made her straighten up. It was a sound she knew, furtive as fox or rabbit creeping through the starched grass: the leaves had begun to fall. They fell from elm and beech, from lime and sycamore, they fell straight down through the still air, but with no haste. It was as if each leaf—green or yellow, brown or spotted grey—paused before relinquishing its hold, and this pause gave Miss Everton the impression that the pale sun had been a signal, was in fact their puppet master. Fascinated, she watched their regulated ballet, their unregretful, unhurried surrender. The patter increased, the tempo seemed to quicken, the air was full of falling leaves.

"Excuse me, could we get any water from the cottage? Are you the owner?"

At the sound of a human voice Miss Everton turned her head unwillingly. A young man stood by her side, also staring at the trees. He watched one or two leaves drop twirling from the sycamore, hesitating before they settled on the chastened grass. "It's all a matter of contraction and expansion, I suppose," he went on. She noticed he wore leather leggings and was obviously in charge of the working party.

"Yes, it's my cottage. There's a tap in the garden you can use." She purposely ignored his explanation, wanting him to go as quickly as possible. So few people called on her that when someone did it was intolerable. All the same, she could not help adding that she used the garden tap to water her flowers. She was proud of her water supply, achieved after much fuss, piped from the hill right into her house.

"I'd be grateful if we could use it to water some less attractive objects," said the young man, jerking his head towards the prisoners, who now stood with picks and shovels in the middle of the field. "Still, they're better than Italians any day. All song and no work, those 'tallies. Now I wouldn't call the Jerries exactly cheerful, but—"

"I'll show you where the tap is." Miss Everton said, and led the way to the cottage. The young man shrugged, beating his legs with a switch. He was only trying to be friendly, on a job like this a friendly woman, even if she was middle-aged, could make a lot of difference. But Miss Everton was not feeling friendly. She did not like the young man's voice, nor the things he said. It was useless to tell herself that he was young, and only the young could ally with their innocence a certain cynicism, a certain brash cruelty that supported them, seeing as they did the world falling in pieces around them. Also, he had probably seen the Germans under very different circumstances, and to have them (or a cross-section of them) under his command was an uncomfortable experience. The thrill for him had undoubtedly been in the chase, not the capture. As he tested the tap, and talked on with that touch of a ringmaster's arrogance, Miss Everton began to fathom his feelings towards the prisoners; it was a sort of distorted pity, which made him despise both them and himself.

Later that morning, when the day had settled down to its accustomed autumnal chill, alleviated by thin sunshine, she heard the water hum and sing through the pipes. Startled, for she had become absorbed in her housework, she peered out of an upstairs window and saw two of the prisoners drawing water. She did not go downstairs, but stayed watching them as they straightened up and went out of the gate, pulling it shut after them. She noticed that the taller of the two looked searchingly at the cottage before following his companion across the field. The thought occurred to her that even if they tried to escape, they could not get very far, the round yellow patches on their uniforms stood out as clearly as targets.

When they had disappeared she prepared her lunch, but she was restless. How long were they going to be there? How many times a day would her gate click open and the pipes hum and sing as the prisoners drew water? It was more than disturbing, they were too near altogether, only a field away. She knew that the thought of them working in the cold would hang like a shadow over her own work—doubtless she would hear whistles marking their rest periods; twice a day the lorries would roar past.

Tomorrow she would speak to them. All the afternoon she rehearsed a few German phrases, wanting to hand them out, like comforts, to the silent men. After all, they were not of her generation, she had known an older Germany; lustier, lusher, more prosperous: gayer. As a girl she and her brother Humphrey had gone off on trips together—he had studied at Bonn and she had picked up a good deal of slangy, everyday talk, although she had never been able to carry on much of a discussion in the language. But then she had never had much occasion to argue—the young men she met did not argue with women. They merely danced with them, walked with them, made sentimental love to them. How did these poor fellows manage? She found herself half turning to ask Humphrey about it, and his loss came once more as a bitter pain. She missed more than anything, now she was nearing fifty, not having anyone to whom she could say "Do you remember?" For at this moment she was remembering acrid black coffee at Aachen at one o'clock in the morning, drunk from cardboard cups. Shutting her eyes, she recalled exactly the chill of the platform as the train halted for ten minutes or so before pulling over the border. How cold she had been! That, and the crumpled, sour feeling of travelling all night, had remained as one of her most vivid recollections of the holiday. She scarcely remembered now the rocky islands of the Rhine, rising out of a dawn that would have seemed more real on the stage of Covent Garden, with barbaric and hysterical music uniting the boxes to the gallery.

At four o'clock, settled down over her books and typewriter, Miss Everton heard the pipes sing once more. She did not move. Her lips rehearsed a greeting, but she could not bring herself to go to them—what if they looked at her dumbly, with dislike or amusement? Still she sat on, knowing that soon they would be gone for the day and the opportunity of showing them that someone in this cold northern corner of England had known the dark-green Harz mountains, and the gentle Bavarian country, would be lost. Sure enough, half an hour later, she heard a thin whistle and soon after the lorries churned past. She was grateful for the garden wall and the thick trees around the cottage—terrible if the men could gaze in the window and see her sitting there, lonely over her tea.

Leaving the teapot warming by the fire, Miss Everton suddenly rose up, called Tag, and together they went across the tightening ground in the falling light. She stopped by the big tree in the middle of the field. The fire was still smouldering. On either side a sharpened stake stood erect, the top shaped like a catapult. Across this the men evidently laid another stick and hung their tins from it over the flames. She smiled. That was clever, it really was! Somehow it made the whole thing seem like a game, played with the same absorption as boy scouts on a camping holiday. It reminded her of the gipsies of two summers ago; she had often watched the caravans, floating like lighted boats on the rising ground mist of early September.

The blackened tins swung from the tree above her making dry sounds in the slight wind. Neatly cut logs and twigs were piled ready for the next day: picks and other tools were stacked round the tree. Across the fields stretched a line of stakes; they must have spent the day measuring out the lines of ditches to be dug. Miss Everton shivered. Calling Tag, she returned home.

The evenings had once been her dread. Together, as they had been for so many years, she and Humphrey had defeated the weariness and claustrophobia forced on them by the grey lowering skies or close darkness of winter, by reading aloud to each other. They had chosen passages to fit the mood of the elements. On stormy nights Humphrey would read about the old gossips at the bar of the *Maypole* and of poor Barnaby Rudge, who had in him the sweetness of some of Shakespeare's fools. Summer evenings called for something more serene, prose that pleased the mind, so they chose Conrad's *Typhoon* (for Humphrey longed for the sea and the tropics) or Lamb's lucid dissertations. This last choice was Miss Everton's; she longed to reach back through the years and comfort

Lamb, seeing in his devoted life something akin to her own and her brother's.

Humphrey, too, liked to think that their relationship was also serenely echoed by Wordsworth and his sister Dorothy, and he never failed, on the first suitable spring day, to quote William's charming poem written to Dorothy. It began, 'It is the first mild day of March', and he would walk round the cottage and tap on the kitchen window, doffing his knitted woollen cap to declaim, with further courtly gestures:

> My sister! (Tis a wish of mine)
> Now that our morning meal is done,
> Make haste, your morning task resign,
> Come forth, and feel the sun.
>
> Then come, my sister, come, I pray,
> with speed put on your woodland dress
> and bring no book: for this one day
> We'll give to idleness.

Their lives had been full of such small pleasures. Orphaned early, given over to the uncaring care of aunts (which made both bookish children appreciate keenly Saki's stories, and take an almost proprietorial interest in Augustus Hare and the young Kipling) they had never felt any strong desire to allow anyone else within their private world. After childhood, the door remained shut.

When Humphrey died—in the third year of the war, from pneumonia contracted by crawling through wet bracken on a useless Home Guard foray—she had not known what to do. Her sense of loneliness was so complete, so terrible that all sense of the division between night and day went from her. Her mind and body knew only coldness; she was consumed by the fear of going mad. She was one of those people to whom the Bible was a habit and not a consolation, and she lacked the pure courage to follow philosophical thought; that way was too bare, too cold.

She supposed that the larger part of life was habit, after all, was question and answer, so that one's mind and body were put off balance by a sudden, eternal absence of response. Would she have mourned a husband so bitterly? Once she had been sought after, but not passionately, and in her bereavement she sometimes remembered those glances and fleeting caresses, but neither name nor face of the young man. Shoddy emotions! One must hold oneself back from that sort of loose and undefined loving.

She found her comfort in the village people. Living as they did with the churchyard in the centre of the village, with birth and death as inevitable as the spring and the fall of the year, they had a melancholy and yet unquestioning acceptance. This attitude at last seeped into Mary Everton's plunging mind and steadied her: she felt, after many months, a deeper sense of life itself. The next thing was to accustom herself to a new routine, for it was the small daily setting forth of one cup instead of two, of one bed to make, a smaller batch of weekend cakes, that troubled her.

But gradually she found another interest, one that was closely connected with Humphrey. She had always lent books to one or two of her friends, and had taken pleasure in suiting the book to the person. Now she went further; she started a small library in the village. With the co-operation of the Women's Institute she enrolled subscribers and went round buying books cheaply and begging volumes from friends' libraries. Slyly she introduced the village women to authors they had not read since leaving school. She widened her own reading and passed on her preferences to the others. She was adviser and secretary as well as librarian and treasurer. The work filled her evenings and she began to feel content.

This was the rhythm the coming of the German prisoners interrupted. It threw her out of key, so that instead of checking the library lists after her light supper (she combined tea and supper, boiling or poaching an egg each evening), she sat down and thought about the men who had arrived that day. She sighed, and shifted in her little low chair—for she was not a tall woman and liked to stretch out her legs before the fire—and wondered if their advent would upset her. She wished they would go away.

II

The cold set in with a new moon. The air seemed to contract, and the Germans went about the fields with a hunched, defensive walk, as if their flesh prickled with cold under the thick, rough khaki. They blew into their hands and beat their arms, they drew breath cautiously, as if it pained them to gulp down the icy, knife-sharp air. They returned reluctantly to their digging after their brief rests by the fire. In the middle of this cold snap a small hut appeared. A lorry brought it one morning. It had two central wheels and the men propped it up on tree trunks to keep it steady.

Miss Everton, watching shamelessly through her bedroom window, saw that it had a chimney and a window and a decent door. She was pleased, thinking that the men could eat their dinner in the warm. She knew two of them by name, for a few days ago one of them had knocked softly on her kitchen window, asking for a cardboard box. She had been startled, disconcerted; it was a signal from the cold, a challenge from the outcast. They watched each other through the closed, frosted window in that moment's hesitation; a solidly built young man and a small, ordinary looking woman with a face like a startled mouse. She had given him an old shoe box and he went away; someone called him from the field. Erich.

Miss Everton went downstairs and busied herself with her cooking. She was mashing potatoes when she heard that soft knock again. This time she went to the door, and opened it. It was the same young man, his face red with cold. He held out a paper bag, full of something.

"You want tea?" he asked.

"Please come in," she said, to gain time. He stepped inside gingerly, hauling his cap from his head. Once the door was shut he stood awkwardly, like a horse led to a new stable, his great rubber boots thick with mud and ice. His mild blue eyes were fixed on the bright coal fire and the steaming saucepan of potatoes, his hands were tough and weathered as a ploughboy's.

"Tea," he said again, offering her the bag. She looked puzzled, and in explanation he went on, "The chaps want to ask if you will give coffee in exchange." His English was careful, free of mistakes; he had obviously been going over the words in his head. It seemed odd to her that the prisoners should be referred to as chaps—it was too free and easy, too English.

"*Bitte setzen Sie hier,*" murmured Miss Everton, pushing a chair up to the fire. She poured a cup of tea, for she had just made herself one as was her mid-morning custom, and handed it to him. He looked up at her with slight pleasure, although he did not comment on her German. She went to the larder and took out a two-pound tin of coffee and laid it on the table. Surely it wasn't illegal? No, she told herself firmly, exchange was perfectly legal. Also, she was often short of tea: one person living alone suffered worst from rationing.

She began to ask him questions; about himself, about his family. He told her he came from Saxony, from a small farm; now he wanted to go back to look after his mother. He did not seem to fear the fact that he would be living in the Russian zone. But Russians filled her with dread, she saw them as half-human, rampaging through smoking cities, snatching at women and wrist-watches indiscriminately.

"What do we Germans deserve, anyway?" said Erich, seeing her shudder.

But Miss Everton could not believe in this kind of humility. It did not match her own experience. It was intensely embarrassing to hear such a thing said—unless, of course, it was meant as mordant humour, directed as much against her as against himself. This helpless air, this ghost of self-pity annoyed her. She felt sure that no Englishman in the same situation would have allowed these sentiments to creep into his attitude. But then, she told herself quickly, the English would never have allowed themselves to be defeated.

Erich thoughtfully laid down his cup. "Yes," he said. "Yes, you are kind. I find good people wherever I go. In Canada, in South Wales—all good people if you look for them …" He seemed puzzled at the thought of there being so many good people about, and yet the world itself being so unsatisfactory. "We drink tea plain at the barracks," he said suddenly, "but it is nice with sugar and milk."

Miss Everton could not imagine anyone drinking tea like that. She had to query it.

"We save our sugar to cook with, and the milk is in tins," he explained. "We don't bring any to work in the fields."

"But you have a nice warm hut to eat your dinner in," said Miss Everton, trying to be cheerful, and feeling that a prisoner ought not to complain.

"Hut? Oh ..." He looked at her with his face closed up into what, on subtler features, would be wryness. "That is for the overseer, and for the papers and the tea. That is not for us."

There was a tap at the window and he swung round. "That is Kurt. I go at once, they are asking for me." He took up the coffee and ducked his head. "*Danke schoen,* tomorrow we talk again." And he was gone.

After that Erich called in often. Sometimes they had biscuits with their mid-morning cup of tea. She asked about his family, and learnt that his father was dead, that he sent his mother parcels when he could, that on the whole he was disappointed with England, finding it dirty and unfriendly. Miss Everton grew attached to him, as one does to a tentative mongrel dog or a small child, and humoured him, giving him sweet things to eat—as if her gifts could somehow assuage the times in which he had been born. Although she scarcely admitted it to herself, these small offerings—some coffee, or a tinned pudding or stew for his mother—helped to smother a niggling, inexplicable feeling of shame. She noticed that he never asked any questions about herself, and at first thought it was because of the barrier his imprisonment raised between them. Then she began to see, as the weeks passed and his mind became more familiar to her, that although he might discuss the outside world with her, to him other people's lives were like glimpses from a slow-moving train. One passed small gardens; in one a woman was putting her baby out in a pram, in another a man bent over his onion bed, children ran in and out of doorways like silverfish on a hearth. These were brief glimpses only, they offered no clue to the constant stream of life flowing away from the train, gave nothing but a temporary warmth. Erich dared not be too interested, possessing as he did the bewildered, blunted mind of the uprooted peasant.

There was one question Miss Everton wanted to ask him, however, and one day she did. How had he been captured? He told her quite simply that he had been in a submarine which had surrendered. Encouraged and forced on by something urgent in her own nature, Miss Everton asked in a voice that grew thin with embarrassment—as if she were committing a social gaffe—whether it was true that U-boat captains surfaced after destroying an enemy ship and shot all survivors.

He sat playing with her broken potato peeler, then said simply, "Men do terrible things in a war; I have thought a lot about it."

"Did you, did your captain shoot our men?" demanded Miss Everton again, her body growing cold.

Erich roared with laughter, watching her as he did so. "We never hit a ship," he replied. "I was only at sea for a year and we seemed to go sailing up and down the coast of South America."

"But why?"

"We were getting sunk, and U-boats don't like that. We were given a go-slow order." He laughed again, as if cajoling her, then stood up, slipping the peeler into his pocket. "See, I take this away and mend it for you."

III

As the days drew nearer to Christmas the sun begun to shine frostily, and Miss Everton often felt the need for a walk. But the usual one she took across the fields out to the farm, there to have a chat and a cup of tea with Mrs. Jones, the farmer's wife, was now blocked by the line of extending and deepening ditches. Rolls of barbed wire lay at various points, ready to put into position as soon as the stakes were up. Looking out from her bedroom window at the number of men digging, she felt her first active pang of resentment since the lorries had first roared up across the fields. She, in effect, was the prisoner; the sun glinted on barbed wire, heaps of thrown-up earth glittered frostily. The fields were no longer free; she was watched wherever she went, once outside the protective walls of her garden. She did not fear the men, her unease was for herself—unwilling participant in their forced labour—and how they might change her very nature.

Erich mended her potato peeler, and when he brought it back handed her a present as well. A pair of bedroom slippers made out of an unravelled, dyed and plaited sack. He had sewn on leather soles, and added large bobbles at each centre front. Miss Everton was as much touched by the ugliness of his gift as by the patient and ingenious work that had gone into the making of it. When he showed her some bracelets he had made out of some sort of plastic material, she offered to sell them for him in the village. It would bring him in a little extra money for Christmas.

One morning he came to the window with a request. He asked whether she had any maps of South Wales—his friends there had asked him to spend the holiday with them. They were small farmers and he had worked on their land for a while; he told her that they had been like parents to him. Christmas was a family festival, *nicht wahr*? If the distance was within the hundred-mile limit he would be allowed to go. Miss Everton, feeling his excitement as a personal thing, searched upstairs for a map and brought it down.

They spread it out on the table, looking for Pembrokeshire. It was worn and frayed at the folds, but still legible. With a ruler they measured out distances.

"Yes," said Miss Everton at last, touched by the sight of those large fingers going tenderly over the names of places where he had once been able to make friends, "It looks to me as if you might just be able to go."

"Ah," Erich straightened up, his eyes almost sparkling. "To go on a train alone, live in a house with a fire for two whole days, sleep without twenty other men—now that would be *wunderbar.*"

As he left he whistled a little folk tune down the path, his boots crunching in the light fall of frozen snow. Next day he was back again.

"So," he said, stamping the snow off his boots before he came inside the back door. "I cannot go. I ask the railway station to make sure, and we go over it, the stationmaster and I. It is twenty miles too far. I must stay in camp." His eyes had a cold, disappointed look. Miss Everton was sure that he was determined not to complain, not to make a fool of himself and his hopes, or to parade his misery.

For the first time she fully approved of him; a man should be in control of his feelings. She asked him briskly what they did in camp at Christmas time, and he told her in a cold, formal voice that they saved up for a good dinner and might have a concert in the evening. At home there would be a little tree and the cradle with the Child in it—his little sister would make a rag doll—and they might still be using the figures he had carved before the war. Yes, he had carved Mary and Joseph and the three kings, while his father had carved the shepherds and some of the animals. Only, this year there would be no sugar sweets to hang on the tree. Of course his mother may be able to make small biscuit rings. She would think of something. But Erich did not stay long. It seemed as if he identified Miss Everton, too, with the authority that spoilt his Christmas, and the drumming consciousness that he was a prisoner made any easy talk impossible. He left the cottage without his usual cup of tea.

That evening, when she was alone, instead of working on the accounts—she had neglected the library lately—Mary Everton sat and thought about him. She was grateful for the mended peeler and the gift of shoes, but they made her uneasy. In a strange way she felt bound to do more for him in return. From purely humanitarian motives she ought to ask him to spend Christmas with her. But what would the village people say, how would Mrs. Jones feel about it? Mrs. Jones had already asked her to spend Christmas Day with them, and she had accepted. She clung to this fact as she debated the reasons for and against. But wasn't it her duty to make at least one other person happy when the opportunity arose? There was little enough she could do about the callousness of the world; she ought then, surely, to try and improve her small corner of it. But what when he had gone, swallowed up in the Russian Zone? She would have to continue to live among the villagers, who never forgot anyone's departure from their accepted code. No, it was out of the question. Even though he was young enough to be her son.

The next day she caught the early bus into the nearest market town. The shops were decorated. In the largest one a woman disguised as Father Christmas stood at the door and stamped her feet, occasionally lifting her cotton wool beard to carry on a conversation with a passing acquaintance. This shocked Miss Everton profoundly, thinking of the bitter disillusion such an action would have on any trusting child brought up to believe in Father Christmas. She carried on with her Christmas shopping, goods were beginning to be available again, and she spent more than she had intended. She had lunch and went to the pictures in the afternoon. But even as she watched the screen, flickering into momentary life in black and white, she wondered what Erich would think if he had come to the window that morning and found her away. She clasped her parcels as if to excuse herself, for in one of them was an expensive warm scarf and a pair of gloves for him, a jumper for his mother, socks for his sister, and a small box fitted with sewing materials. She was buying him gifts, so why did she feel uncomfortable, unaccountably mean? Oh, she would be glad when they had all gone! The parked lorries, the overseer's hut, the barbed wire, the prisoners spread silently over the fields—all gone to some other part of the country. It wasn't fair, this intrusion.

The next day the first person she saw was the young overseer. As usual, he was rinsing out his mug at the tap. Miss Everton would associate the tap with him long after he was gone.

"Well," he said, watching as she shook out her kitchen mat, "we'll be off before Christmas after all. Leave you in peace then. Some of this lot will be home in the Fatherland in the new year; things are speeding up. We leave here Christmas Eve." He added grudgingly, "They've done a good job."

Miss Everton's cold hands dropped the mat, mechanically she slapped Tag as he tried to worry the strings of her apron. "Christmas

Eve," she repeated slowly. "Why, that's the day after tomorrow. So you've finished, then?"

He looked at her jauntily. "That's right," he said. Miss Everton went indoors. She took stock of her larder, then started to mix a cake. It was ready for the oven when Erich came for water with another man. He smiled and waved but did not come in. Perhaps he was keeping away because he could not bear her to talk to him in her usual friendly way and not ask him the one thing he wanted to hear. Tears came to her eyes as she put the cake in the oven.

The following morning she iced it, first putting a thick layer of almond paste on the top, made with soya flour and almond flavouring, which was the best she could do. She found she was talking aloud to herself. "After all," she said, smoothing the paste with a rolling pin, "when our men were prisoners, the farmers' wives gave them basins full of mashed turnips to eat, like animals. Humphrey would agree, I'm sure. I can't do it—even for the sake of the holidays we had over there. When you're young you can be happy anywhere; it's stupid to feel so guilty, so heavy-hearted about it." At least, she told herself, he should have his cake with a miniature Father Christmas on the top. And some mince pies. With all the shortages, that was a sacrifice in itself.

She put the cake in the larder and went outside to cut a sprig of holly from her hedge. It was then she realised that if Erich came she would have to put him in Humphrey's room—in Humphrey's bed. She must be mad even to consider such a thing. A stranger! And what would they talk about all day? Two days? One got out of the habit of sustained conversation, living alone. Now if Humphrey were alive ... she saw the three of them sitting round the fire, recalling a Germany Erich had not known, being too young. They would recreate his country for him; the walking, the swimming, the songs, the dancing. Briefly she hummed to a memory of concertinas in the beer gardens, the churning swing of:

Wenn am Sonntag Abend
Die Dorfmusik spielt ...

If Humphrey were alive they would sing carols softly, and make Erich a gift of innocence.

Miss Everton caught herself up sharply. This would never do. Innocence indeed. How innocent? Violence and fury had been the fourth, invisible gift at that birth in the stable. Gold, frankincense, myrrh and the sword, like a curse laid by the wicked fairy uninvited to the feast. Just as violence and fury had lain all about those halcyon days, unsuspected. She was a fool to imagine that she could wave the good-fairy-wand. Such a role, she told herself with wry disgust, ill became her. It was *ersatz,* a word that summed up a great deal of the war.

The next day he came to see her for the last time.

"Today is Christmas Eve," he said, and on his tongue the words were heavy with nostalgia, with an ancient tradition of goodwill and kindliness. "I want to thank you for all you have done, it has meant a lot to me. I have to say goodbye now." He hesitated, "In a month or less I go back to Germany."

"Do you really want to go back?" she asked. "Couldn't you—" She caught a look on his face as he glanced sharply at her. She finished lamely, "couldn't you stay over here somehow?"

"How? My father dead, my mother growing old, with a farm to see to? She needs me with her." After a pause he went on, with a trace of disbelief, "Anyway, there may be some good Russians who will let me work on in peace. I am lucky with people. After all, we are all separate men and women, no? We each think with our own heads and feel with our own hearts, whatever salute our hands must give." He put down his cup, for his hands were trembling. "Miss Everton, do you believe in God?"

She was startled by the urgency in his voice. His words spurted up like hot springs from boiling depths. She felt he wanted to stand up and smash something, cry out with anguish at his situation. It was the kind of despair that the English were saved from, a despair that had always racked Europe and showed itself in suicide pacts, created great literature. It was there in Erich's tormented lumpiness, his heavy head now bowed over her kitchen table. Staring at him, she felt a terrifying sense of inadequacy, of rage at her own small and withered emotions, which—far from being red hot and turbulent—were merely anchored like icebergs one third above the surface of a cold sea. Self-discipline could be a kind of death.

Being a woman, alone, with her own life to live, she went briskly to the larder

"Of course I believe in God," she said severely, as if amazed that such a question could be asked. "He works in an inscrutable way. He tests each of us to the limit of our endurance. Now here is a cake I have baked for you, and some mince pies." Let these comfort him where I cannot. She displayed the cake for him to see before packing it into a box, then she left him and hurried from the kitchen. In her sitting-room was an array of parcels, wrapped in coloured paper and tied with tinsel string, each labelled. She picked up two of them, and went back to Erich. He was regarding the cake with serious, melancholy eyes.

"I hope—I—*fröhliche Weinachten*!" she said in a rush, and tumbled the presents into his hands. It was obvious that he did not know what to say. He just clasped them to him and looked up at her. A tap at the window saved them from the embarrassment of thanks and protestations, and hurriedly Miss Everton began parcelling up the cake and the mince pies, telling him to share them with his friends if he wanted to, and to wish them all a happy Christmas from her.

At the door they said goodbye. Miss Everton held out her hand, but he had difficulty in clasping it because he was so laden. On impulse she stood on tiptoe and kissed him gently on the cheek. "God bless you," she said, and closed the door.

She stood and looked at it for a long time, then went quietly to her room and took down her hair before the mirror. As she brushed it with long practised strokes tears flowed down her cheeks; she could not stop them. It became a desolate rhythm, the strokes of the brush against her long soft hair and the tears chasing down her cheeks. Usually this ritual of hair-brushing soothed her when she felt her nerves tight and jangled, but it was a long time before it had that effect today. She could not push away the picture of Erich looking in at other people's Christmases through their lighted windows. At last, exhausted and cold, she lay on her bed, pulling the eiderdown over her, and stared out of the window. Tag was whining at the door, doubtless the fire would be low; she dropped into an unhappy day sleep.

She didn't know at first what had awakened her. Here was her room, the rumpled bedclothes that did not belong to the neutral light of a winter afternoon. Then she gradually realized what she was listening to—the harsh, growing throb of engines preparing to move off. She knew this sound so well that she did not really need to stumble to the window to watch the lorries moving off for the last time. The little hut bowled along behind on its two wheels.

She felt a panicky desire to shout after them. Although she knew that within a month or two the men moving off would be facing conditions that she, and everyone else in this country, would find intolerable, it seemed to her that they were free, and once again she the imprisoned one.

She went downstairs, thinking to make herself a cup of tea, but the heavy silence and the sullen fire defeated her. She called Tag, reproachfully half asleep on the mat, nose down to his paws, and together they left the cottage. A few minutes later she was contemplating the blackened tins hanging from the large beech tree, the still warm ashes of the fire, and the deep raw ruts the wheels had torn in the frozen earth. Not one of the prisoners had had the heart to cut his initials into the tree. That sort of gesture sprang from happiness, from a desire to remember and be remembered. As it was, all marks of them would soon be gone; ashes scattered, ruts grown over with bright spring grass, the tins and few cut sticks seized by questing children. If she excepted the ditches, with the glinting barbed wire and straight, deep sides, along which water already tinkled, things would soon be just as if they had never come. And, after all, ditches could be dug by anybody, anybody at all.

She went on telling herself this until she was indoors again, raking up the fire, putting on a kettle. It was not until she sat at her desk to face the library lists, a cup of tea beside her, that she threw down her pen and put her head in her hands. For she knew that nothing, no, nothing at all, would ever be the same again.

THE CUT FINGER

Frances Bellerby

One day not long after Christmas they said to the five-year-old child: "Judith, would you like to go and stay at the seaside? Just the three of us, when Nicholas has gone back to school."

"Well, I think I would," she replied, going to the window. A stranger would probably have thought her uninterested.

The truth was that the idea astounded and overwhelmed her. It was too new to be accepted with equanimity, too far outside her experience actual or imaginative. It had never been realised by Judith that the seaside continued beyond the golden stretch of summer holidays. Yet now all in a moment she had to grasp that it was possible to go there when tangerines, tinsel and holly were still realities; when the days were grey and cold, the trees without leaves; and when—as they sat at breakfast in the lighted room with the fresh, clear, merry fire in the grate—the trams bumping past outside were gaily illuminated in the prolonged night.

And there was another startling innovation to be considered. Only three would be going to the seaside. Not Nicholas.

Presently Judith, heavy with thought, went to find her eight-year-old brother. She guessed where he'd be, and there he was: alone in the scullery, peeling potatoes with the peeler he had given cook for Christmas. Judith watched in silence for a few moments, then said in a stiff way: "When you've gone back to school we're going to the seaside."

Nicholas didn't look up. Two potatoes had been done without breaking the peel. A third would make the hat-trick. He spoke through clenched teeth. "I know. Mother told me. Lucky dogs. Instead of mouldy old Latin grammar and beetles in the tea."

By this Judith at once knew that he didn't mind at all; that he was longing for his second term to begin quite as much as he was enjoying every minute of the Christmas holidays. She noticed too the pride and satisfaction with which he peeled the potato.

So out poured her eager questions, for there was nobody like Nicholas for answering any and every question she ever asked.

"I didn't know people went to the seaside in winter, did you? Why will we go? Will we have a boat? Will we take sandwiches in the train? Will we bathe if it's ice?"

Nicholas said loudly: "Oh well played, sir! Hat-trick, by Jove!" And he bowled the potato with an overarm action into a bowl of water. Carefully selecting another, he then replied to his sister.

"Of course people go to the seaside in winter if they're ill or something. It's to make Daddy well, didn't you even know *that?* Who'd row you in a boat? You couldn't take a boatman with you like babies. Anyway, you're not going to Looe, you're going to Haven, and of course you won't take sandwiches in the train when it's only fifteen miles away, as a matter of fact there was a man who lived on nothing but water for sixty-three days, so now do you understand? And there isn't ice on the sea but of course you won't bathe in January. Now help me wipe up the floods, as you're here."

Judith did his bidding, all her difficulties swept away, her mind happily adapted to the new situation.

Later, she pondered the word "Haven" and what it might contain. The place was unknown to her. Indeed, she had thought "the seaside" to be simply another name for Looe; but the scrap of fresh knowledge could be quickly absorbed now that her mind no longer staggered in bewilderment; quickly, too, she absorbed the idea that they were going to Haven for the purpose of making Daddy well again, and this idea made a splash of bright colour in her mind. The "poor Daddy" attitude had been right, the acceptable, for long enough to dull her first daily expectation that tomorrow would restore the old, happier attitude. But very easily now, having heard the good news from Nicholas, she recalled essential fragments of that permanent "Daddy": tearing out of the house as the tram bumped past, racing after it, leaping on, turning with a sweeping bow to his cheering family at the window whilst the conductor grinned resignedly. Singing *Old soldiers never die* and *The Mountains of Mourne* in the bathroom. Putting the tea-cosy on his head and prancing into the room to kneel at Mother's feet and present her with a cauliflower. Sitting on a chair with his legs crossed behind his neck as the vicar's wife came up the path, and pretending to Mother that he'd got stuck. Telling stories, reading poetry, by firelight to Mother, Nicholas and Judith—beautiful stories and poetry, strangely fascinating, deeply real, holding the three so-different people as if in a magic circle. …

For days Judith remained almost completely silent, absorbed in her inner life, luminous with thought.

⁂

Haven wasn't in the least like Looe. The most salient quality about this new seaside was its greyness. A clean, smooth, washed greyness, like beach-stones. Occasionally, it is true, the sea changed itself to a deep pinkish-brown, and the foam of the broken waves became coffee-coloured. And against the grey sky gulls soared, to drift as though in a dream, flashing whiteness as they tilted, leaning on the air. And far out on the lustreless sea white horses tossed their manes in wild glory.

But the roads were grey, the houses were grey, the rocks were grey. The wind was grey; and salty grey—like a licked seashore pebble—tasted the cold air in one's mouth.

Judith loved everything deeply.

In the mornings she and her mother went shopping whilst her father stayed in bed. They walked along the quiet grey road with a pine-wood on one side and on the other side the low gentle cliff and the sea. They passed a solitary shop, very clean: a dairy. And went on to the shopping street of the small town. Sometimes, when they had finished in the shops, they walked down to the sea-front and along the empty esplanade, and made up stories about the neat little houses in a row facing the sea; every house was so neat and precise, yet no two were exactly alike, which delighted Judith. When the tide was far out there was a wide stretch of mud beyond the flat seaweedy rocks, and sometimes, though the sun never came out properly, this mud glinted and glimmered as though lanterns were being shone down on it from behind the clouds. Judith's mother said that mud was one of the things that made the place so good for people who had been ill; it put the right things into the air for them to breathe. But in any case Judith would have liked the mud.

On the way back the two always paid a visit to the lonely dairy, which sold special cakes and biscuits, and also sugar almonds in four colours: pink, white, blue, amethyst. Smooth and delicate in shape, and with their frail evanescent colours, these sweets seemed of all others the perfect ones to fit the *whole* situation in which Judith found herself at Haven. Sight, touch, taste, were deeply satisfied.

Back in the landlady's cosy house—which stood by itself but quite near other small houses—Judith's mother would go to give the things for lunch to the younger Miss Pearson, whilst Judith kept her father company. He would be downstairs by now, in the big chair by the fire. They talked, or played Snap or Noughts and Crosses, or drew pictures for one another. Then the younger Miss Pearson would come in to lay lunch. Judith thought both sisters remarkably pretty, with their pink faces and blue eyes and silvery hair. She couldn't see how one could be elder, one younger; to her they looked exactly the same size, but the difference was that one was good at cooking and the other wasn't, so they did different things. They called one another "Sister".

After lunch Judith rested on her bed upstairs, and her father on the sofa downstairs, and her mother read or mended their clothes by the fire. Then, if it wasn't too cold, they all went for a short walk. Usually they went as far as the edge of the pine-wood, where there was a seat, and there the grown-ups rested whilst the child played about. When the father had rested long enough they went slowly home again to gas-lit tea in the little, full room with the bright fire made up ready for them. The lacy white cloth would be laid cornerwise on top of the thick red cloth with the bobbled fringe, the heavy red curtains would be drawn across the windows and the door. Judith's father always lay on the sofa after his walk.

Sometimes, though, the afternoons were different. It would be too cold or too windy for Judith's father to go out. Then her mother would stay in to read to him, whilst the child played alone in the Pearson sisters' garden. She always found plenty to do. Her father had often said that was why she was so quiet—because she was so intensely busy, perhaps busiest of all when she stayed perfectly still! People frequently remarked on her quietness.

The garden was interesting to Judith. Very neat and arranged in front, with two tiny lawns and a pebble-path between, and a strip of earth under the privet hedge and railings. But round at the back things could hardly have been more different. Brushes and boxes lay about, and bits of things waiting, perhaps, to be mended. There was a tree, too, which the sisters said was an apple-tree, but the rough grass around it was scattered with nothing but brown stiff leaves. There was also a place which looked like a sentry-box such as Nicholas's toy soldiers had, but was a kind of lavatory; its roof was orange-coloured with rust. There was also a pump with a small stone trough under it.

One afternoon Judith was surprised to hear that her parents were not going out. The day was as usual grey, but windless, and far warmer than the weather they had been having. "Really a feeling of Spring in the air!" the younger Miss Pearson said with gentle triumph as she laid the lunch. And she bestowed on the young people and their little girl the shy blessing of her quick, nervous, compassionate smile. But in spite of all this Judith's father felt too tired that day to go for a walk.

So Judith went into the garden. First, she chose six pebbles from the path. It was the striking individuality of everything in the world which most delighted and enthralled Judith. When the pebbles had been chosen she took them with her round the house to the back garden, and made her way to the pump. This was her favourite place. It was private, too, for the house only had windows in front and at one side, and from the walled back garden other houses were not in view.

She began to play with the pebbles on the rim of the stone trough, and presently dropped one in by mistake. Pulling up her sleeve, she groped about in the leaf-mouldy water, and at last grasped her pebble and withdrew her hand. Then, with intense excitement, she perceived watery blood colouring one finger. She had cut herself, evidently, on something sharp among the debris on the bottom of the trough!

You couldn't tell much from watery blood, of course, but Judith carefully dried her finger on the grass, and then squeezed—and behold! A dark red bead appeared, swelled, trembled, collapsed, and flowed quite thickly, even dripped when she shook her hand. This really was a cut! She experimented, swishing the finger to and fro in the trough water; almost at once, no blood was to be seen. But as soon as she took her finger out of the water, redness appeared, and even the water didn't spoil it now; and when she raised her hand in the air the redness ran down her wrist under her coat-sleeve.

Then Judith felt a thrill of fear. Not hurtful fear, though, because of course for as long as she could remember she had known the right thing to do with a cut finger: suck it, and go straight to her mother. Even Nicholas acknowledged this to be the right behaviour where a real cut was concerned.

Judith therefore gathered up her pebbles with her free hand, and made for the house, sucking as she went the smooth, thick, dark-tasting blood.

But when she quietly opened the sitting-room door she saw only her father in the room; lying on the sofa, his face turned away from her towards the grey window. Poor Daddy, he *must* be tired for he wasn't even reading. However, in any case he wasn't the person for cut fingers, so she closed the door again and slowly climbed the stairs, wondering if she were beginning to feel sick with all this blood-drinking.

In her parents' bedroom her mother lay across one of the beds, face downwards, *crying*. …

Down the stairs crept the child, sucking fiercely at her finger as if she wished to drain the last drop of blood from it. With the front door shut, the passage was by now almost dark, and she huddled for a few moments against the hanging coats, shivering, staring. But she heard the clink of china from the pantry and knew that a sister would soon come out to light up before getting the tea. The child opened the front door and slipped out, closing it softly behind her.

Everything out here had changed its mood, for whilst she had been in the house dusk had come. Down the road a few lights gleamed dully.

Judith dropped the pebbles into her coat pocket, and then

wrapped her cut finger in her handkerchief, twisting it round and round until however hard she squeezed no red showed through. Then she ran as fast as she could round the house and up the dim back garden to the pump.

By her good friend the pump she stood, sensing the appalling thing she had seen: the sight which had at a blow destroyed the whole familiar world and scattered in ruthless confusion all her trusted values. *Her mother crying.* How *could* such a thing be? What frightful hurt had brought it about? Her mother! The one person to whom Judith had always gone, by right, without shame or doubt, whenever she herself had been broken to tears. This cherishing omnipotence writhing face-downwards on a bed, sobbing into the pillow—so that the whole world, yes, the whole established world, had been blown sky-high and come hurtling down in fragments anyhow, anywhere. And solid, unbreakable laws such as the one about behaviour when one cut a finger, simply couldn't be carried out: the unbreakable *had* to be broken! And if "poor Daddy" had at first seemed a bewildering and grievous phrase, and had never really slithered into place as a household word, what about the inconceivable, the unutterable "poor Mother"? …

Judith stared down at the water in the little trough. Suddenly it changed. It was no longer dirty. In the west a swift wild amber light had torn the grey sky, and from the trough gleamed back this light. The child took the pebbles from her pocket and arranged them with immense care in couples on the rim of the trough. She took great pains in choosing the partners. When at last all was completed to her satisfaction she stood erect and spoke with vigorous defiance, not in her own voice, pretending to be Nicholas. "As a matter of fact, Mother's not poor, I won't have her be poor, so *now* d'you understand?" It sounded well to her ears, and she repeated it with more assurance. But it wouldn't do. She realised it wouldn't do. More than that was needed. And slowly she bent down, and slowly she pushed, with the clumsy bandaged finger, every pebble in turn so that it plopped into the water. When all this was over the child leaned against the pump sobbing as if her heart were broken.

The wild amber light had been very swift, fading almost as quickly as it had come. Judith turned her back on the trough in whose murky water lay her six pebbles, and slowly made her way towards the dark, unfathomed house.

THE THAMES SPREAD OUT

Elizabeth Taylor

Nothing could have been lovelier, Rose thought. For most of the day she stayed on the little balcony, looking out over the flooded fields. Although it was Friday, Gilbert had not come and she was sure now that he would not come, and was shaken with laughter at the idea of him rowing out to her from the railway station, across the river and meadows, bowler-hatted and red with exasperation.

This day was usually her busiest of the week, when she stopped pottering and worked methodically to make the ramshackle villa and herself clean and tidy. By four o'clock she would be ready, and Gilbert, who was punctual over his illicit escapades as with everything else, would soon after drive down the lane. Perhaps escapade was altogether too exciting a word for the homely ways they had drifted into. She fussed over his little ailments far more than his wife had ever done, not because she loved him more, or indeed at all, but because her position was more precarious.

On Saturday mornings he left her, having broken his long journey from the North, as he told his wife. He often thought how furious she would have been if she had known that the break was only twenty miles from London, where they lived.

As soon as he left her on Saturdays, Rose went down to the shops by the station, cashed the cheque he had given her, and bought some little treats for herself to while away the weekend—a few slices of smoked salmon, chocolate peppermint-creams, and magazines. She loved the rest of that day. Gilbert had gone—she could shut herself in and be cosy till he came again.

Only the faintest regrets ruffled her comfort—little faults in herself that depressed her slightly but could easily be rectified later on. She was shamefully lazy, she knew, and self-indulgent. All the time she meant to save money, but never did. Gilbert was not very generous. His Friday nights were expensive and he knew it and very rarely gave Rose a present. She really had nothing.

Her fur coat, which she had worn all day as she leant over the balcony rail watching the seagulls on the floodwater, was shabby and baggy; he had given it to her years ago at the beginning of their liaison when she was still working for him. It was squirrel, and his wife would not have been seen dead in it.

He certainly won't come now, Rose decided, looking at the forsaken water. There had really never been the slightest likelihood of it, and that was just as well, she thought, catching sight of herself in a glass as she was making a cup of tea. A dark band showed at the parting of her golden hair and she had run out of peroxide.

Some young boy had come in a rowing-boat that morning—a Boy Scout, perhaps—and had offered to do her shopping. She had wrapped some money in the shopping-list and let it down in a basket from the bedroom window. Later he had brought back a loaf of bread and some milk, a pound of sausages and cigarettes, a dozen candles. She would have liked a half-bottle of gin, but had not liked to write it down. The peroxide she had quite forgotten.

She made tea on the primus stove Gilbert had bought for their river picnics. These were in July always, when his wife went to stay with her mother in the Channel Islands. Then he moved in with Rose for a whole fortnight; from niggardly motives made love to her excessively, became irritable, felt cramped in the uncomfortable little house and exasperated by the way it was falling to pieces. The primus stove was hardly ever used. It was too often raining, or they were in bed, or both. Rose was afraid it would blow up, but now, with the floodwater in the downstairs rooms, she had to overcome her fears or go without tea.

The sun was beginning to set and she knew how soon it got dark these winter days. She took her cup of tea and went out on to the balcony to watch. Every ten years or so, the Thames in that place would rise too high, brim over its banks and cover the fields for miles, changing the landscape utterly. The course of the river itself she could trace here and there from the lines of willow trees or other landmarks she knew.

Beyond, on what before had been the other bank, a little train was crossing the floods. The raised track was still a foot or two above river level. Puffing along, reflected in the water, it curved away into the distance and disappeared among the poplar trees by the church. There, all the gravestones were submerged, and the inn had the river flowing in through the front door and out of the back.

"Thames-side Venice," a newspaper reporter had called it. The children loved it, and now Rose saw two young boys rowing by on the pink water. The sun had slipped down through the mist, was very low, behind some grey trees blobbed with mistletoe; but the light on the water was very beautiful. The white seabirds scarcely moved and a row of swans went in single file down a footpath whose high railing-tops on either side broke the surface of the water.

Rose sipped her tea and watched, intent on having the most of every second of the fading loveliness—the silence and the reflections and the light, and then the silence broken by a cat crying far away or a shout coming thinly across the cold air.

"I'm glad he didn't come," she said aloud.

At this hour, other men, husbands, those who had not sent their families away, would be returning. The train was at the station and they would take to their boats and row homewards, right up to their staircases, tying up to the newel-post and greeted from above by their children. Rose imagined them all as lake dwellers and hoped that they were enjoying the adventure.

She was curious about her neighbours—the few of them scattered along the river bank. She wondered about them when she passed by on her way to the shops, but she had never spoken to them or been inside their houses, and she had never wished to do so. Her solitariness suited her and her position was too informal. She would not embarrass other people by her situation.

But she made up stories to herself about some of them, especially about the people at the white house nearby who came only at week-ends. They seemed very gay, and laughter and music went on till late on Saturday nights. From where she was, she could just see the eaves of their boat-house sticking out of the river, but the house itself lay farther back and out of sight.

It was growing dark very fast, and the water, a moment or two earlier rosy, whitened as the sun went down. Under the high woods, out of the wind, the fields were frozen, their black and glassy surface littered with broken ice that boys had thrown.

Suddenly, at last, Rose could bear no more. The strangeness overcame her and she went inside and washed her cup and saucer in the bathroom basin and emptied the tea-pot over the banisters into the flooded passageway.

A swan had come in through the front door. Looking austere and suspicious, he turned his head about, circled aloofly, and returned to the garden. It was weird, Rose thought. This was a word she often used. So many things were to her either weird or intriguing.

The sunset, for instance, had been intriguing, but the sudden beginning of the long evening, the swan coming indoors, the smell of the water lying down there was very weird. She drew the curtains across the balcony doors. They would not meet and she clipped them together with a clothes-peg to keep the darkness hidden.

The bedroom was crowded with furniture and rolled-up matting rescued from downstairs, and looked like a corner of a junk shop. Nothing was new or matched another thing. It had all no doubt been bought off old barrows or hunted for in attics, so that the house could be called furnished when it was let. Wicker uncurled from the legs of an armchair and caught Rose's stockings as she passed by, and in the mornings when she made the bed she picked up dozens of blond feathers from the eiderdown.

It was the first time she had ever had a house to herself. After years of living with her married sister, it had seemed wonderful to put the frying-pan on her own stove and fry her own sausages on it, and she had felt a little self-conscious, as if she were playing at keeping house and did so before an audience, as in the imaginary games of her childhood.

For a time she could not be quite natural on her own. Look at me all the way round, from any angle, I really am a housewife. You won't catch me out, she often thought. But no one was ever there but Gilbert, and he, indifferent to the intriguing notion of her keeping house, sat with his back to her and read his pink newspaper.

In the end the magic had gone, she tired of her rôle, and the home was not one, she saw, that anyone could take a pride in, especially this evening, with candlelight making the crowded room macabre.

"I shall never get the place straight afterwards," she said. She talked to herself a great deal nowadays.

She had forgotten the beauty of the flooded landscape and was overcome by wretchedness. The woman at the post office had warned her of the filth the receding water would leave behind, the smell that lingered, the stained walls and woodwork, and doors half twisted off their hinges.

Earlier that week, as she watched the rockery slowly going under, then the lower boughs of shrubs and very soon the higher ones, Rose had felt apprehensive. She had never had any experience in the least like it. Yet, when the worst happened and the house was invaded, perched up above it, enisled, as if she were hibernating in these unusual surroundings, she had begun to feel elated instead.

Her sister, worried to death from reading about the Thames-side Venice in the newspapers, wrote to ask her to stay. The letter had come by boat and was taken up in a basket through the bedroom window. "Roy and I wish you would come back for good, you know that," Beryl had written. The children missed her. They had been told that she had gone away to work, and the same story did for the neighbours, but they were less likely to think it true.

Roy said that his sister-in-law was wasting herself and ruining her chances. Once a girl takes up with married men, he had told his wife, she will find herself drifting from one to the other and she'll never get married herself. This Beryl left out of the letter.

Rose had been frank about her plans but, wary from long practice of secret affairs, had kept Gilbert's name to herself. "The man I'm going out with," she had called him at the beginning, and so she still wrote of him. She would have made someone a good wife, her brother-in-law often said, knowing what men liked. The house was pleasanter when she was there and the children were easier to manage.

A letter must be written to still her sister's fears. All day, Rose had put it off, but now began to look for some writing-paper. The wardrobe door swung open as she crossed the room and she saw her reflection in the blurred glass front. "My hair!" she thought. She had a suspicion that she might be beginning let herself go, a serious mistake for one in her position.

When she had found the paper and a bottle of green ink, she cleared a corner of the table and began to write. "Dear B, you'd laugh if you could see me at this minute."

She glanced round the room and then, smiling to herself began to describe it. She was a born letter-writer, Beryl said, and she tried consciously to display her talent.

The church clock struck seven. The chimes had a different sound, coming across water instead of grassy meadows. She paused, listened, her chin on her hand and her eyes straying to the curtained door. She thought now that she could hear something moving on the water outside and went to the window and parted the curtain.

Below her, she could see two figures in a punt, one standing and using the pole, the other sitting down and fanning torchlight back and forth across the darkness.

"Going next door," she though, as she sat down again and dipped her pen into the ink. "It's up to the second stair now," she wrote, and then had to jump up, to go and see. Last thing at night, first thing in the morning, and a dozen times a day she would go out to the landing to see if the water had risen or fallen.

The house was open to anyone and the keys of the upstairs rooms had long ago been lost. The swan had come in and so might rats. Nervously, she peered over the banisters.

The water was disturbed and was slapping the threshold and swaying against the staircase. She could hear laughter and then a man's voice echoing up the well of the staircase, calling out to ask if she were safe. "Quite safe and well?" the voice persisted. Torchlight ran up the walls and vanished, and a boat grated against some steps outside.

"Yes, I'm all right," she called out. "Who is it?"

"Next door."

The light came bobbing back across the threshold. Holding the torch was a young man, wading carefully through the water, his trousers rolled up above his pale knees. He came to the bottom of the stairs and looked up at her. His smile was the beginning of laughter, and he seemed to be deeply enjoying the novelties of the situation.

"Are you all alone?" he asked. Then he hurried over the indiscretion and, giving her no time to reply, said, "Don't you mind being up there? We saw the light."

She was tempted to say that she did mind. Then perhaps he would come up the stairs and talk to her for a little while. "No, I don't mind," she replied.

"We saw your light," he said again. "I just wondered if you were all right. 'She might be lying there ill for all we know,' I said to Tony." ("Dead," he had really said.) "'We had better make sure,' I said."

They were both a little drunk. So endearing, Rose found this. It was a long time since she had been with anyone who was in the least intoxicated; Gilbert dully carried his drink and often remarked upon the fact.

"We went to get some whisky."

He seemed not to notice the cold, standing there in the icy water.

"What fun," she said. She smiled back at him. As she leant over the banisters, he spotlighted her with the torch and could see the top of her breasts, white against the green of her jersey as she bent towards him.

A jolly nice bosom, he thought. She seemed to be what he and Tony called a proper auntie. I shall bring out the maternal in her, he thought, and between the banister slats examined her pretty legs. So many plump women have slim ankles. He had often noticed this.

"Why don't you come with us?" he said. "I can carry you to the boat."

"Don't be silly. More like I'd have to carry you."

"Well, paddle, then. It's not cold. It's lovely in."

She had put her hand up to her hair, so he knew that she would come; but before, would go through all the feminine excuses about her appearance.

"There's only us," he said. "You look very nice to me. What my brother thinks is of no importance. I can't stand in this water much longer, though." He held out his arms.

"I'll take off my stockings, then."

She went quickly back to her room. When she had rolled off her stockings and put them into her coat pocket, screwed up the top of the ink-bottle, she took up her shoes and blew out the candles. The hardly started letter was left lying on the table.

"I *could* do with a drink," she said. "I didn't like to ask the errand-boy to fetch some gin. Breaking the law, I suppose."

The torchlight led her down the stairs, and there the young man took her shoes from her and put them in his pockets. He steadied her with his arm and she hitched up her skirt and stepped down into the icy water.

"Oh, my God," she gasped and began to giggle, wading on tiptoe towards the doorway.

"Got her?" Tony shouted. He was sitting in the boat, holding on to the rustic-work porch.

If it all comes away in his hands, Gilbert will go mad, Rose thought, smiling in the darkness.

They helped her into the boat, and Tony, letting go of the porch, gave her a cigarette, lighting it first and putting it into her mouth with the intimacy which comes easily in time of peril or exultation.

"You can put your stockings on now," said the young man whom Tony called Roger. "No more paddling. We row straight in through the French windows to the landing-stage at the foot of the stairs."

Tony gave a final push at the rustic-work porch and swung the punt towards the next-door garden. Bottles jingled against one another under the seat, and when Roger had wiped Rose's feet with a damp handkerchief, he reached for a whisky bottle, took off the wrapping-paper, and let it blow away across the water.

"Keep the cold out," he urged Rose, trying to hold the bottle to her lips. "Your teeth are chattering. Never mind, nearly there, and we've a wonderful oilstove going upstairs."

As the boat swayed, whisky trickled over her chin; then she put her hands over his and, steadying them, took a long drink.

"I'll bet she's been a barmaid," thought Roger.

"Jolly boating weather," Tony sang, and the punt slipped over the still water, and the white house next door came into sight.

"Isn't it lovely?" Rose murmured.

"Not to be missed," said Roger.

The next morning she slept late. It was nearly noon before she was properly awake, and any errand-boys who might have called her from below had gone away unanswered. Even when she was wide awake at last, she lay in bed staring at the curtains pinned across the window, striving to remember all she could of the evening before.

In bright moonlight they had brought her home in the boat and their singing must have carried a long way across the water. I don't care if the boat capsizes, she had thought.

When she waded indoors they called good-night; and she went upstairs and, still with wet bare feet, watched from the window until they were out of sight.

Quite clearly across the water, she heard Roger say, "Well, that worked out all right, didn't it?"

A moment later, a gust of laughter came back to her, and she had wondered uneasily if they were laughing at her. But they were high-spirited boys, she reminded herself. They would laugh at anything. Perhaps Tony had let go of the punt pole.

Before her return home, there must have been hours and hours of sitting on the floor and drinking in what they called "Mamma's bedroom". An oilstove threw a shifting daisy pattern on the ceiling, and two pink candles had been burning on the dressing-table—must surely have burnt themselves out.

"How long was I there?" she wondered. "And how did we pass the time?" While it was happening it had seemed one of the loveliest evenings of her life and she was sorry to have forgotten a moment of it.

The peach-coloured bedroom was draped with satin, and a trail of wet footprints went back and forth across the white carpet. Mamma's wedding photograph was on a little table, and Rose had at one point suddenly asked, "Whatever would your mother say about this?" By "this" she meant herself being there, not empty bottles and the cigarette smoke and the dirty glasses.

"We'll clear up afterwards," Roger said. The other bedrooms were full of furniture from downstairs. They had been sent from London to rescue it.

Now it was Saturday morning and she could not walk down to the shops to buy her little week-end treats. Today there was not cheque to cash, and for the first time she realised how much she was at Gilbert's mercy.

She got out of bed and began to search the room for money, found thirty shillings in one bag, some pennies dusty with face powder in another, half a crown in her mackintosh pocket, and a florin in a broken cup on the chest of drawers. She could survive the week until he came again, just as she could survive until Monday on stale bread and the rest of the sausages.

Yes I can survive all right, she told herself briskly, and pulled off her nightgown and began to dress.

A glimpse in the wardrobe mirror as she crossed the room depressed her. She was getting too fat and her sister would see a difference in her.

"But when?" she wondered. There was the unfinished letter on the table. When she had made herself a cup of tea she would make an effort to write it. I shall go on surviving and surviving, and growing fatter and fatter, she thought, and her lips were pressed together and her eyes flickered because she was frightened.

She lit the primus stove and then unpegged the curtains and opened the balcony windows. Outside, a great change had taken place while she slept. The floods were subsiding. Along the bank of the railway tracks she could see grass, and in the garden the tops of the shrubs and bushes had come up for a breath of air and were steaming in the sunshine. She remembered that last night, as the two young men punted away, she heard one of them say, "The water's going down," and she had felt regret, as if a party were nearing its end.

It was going down more rapidly than it had risen, draining away into the earth, evaporating into the air, hastening down gratings. The adventure was nearly over and in its diminuendo had been an exasperation. What had been so beautiful yesterday was now an inconvenience, and Rose, on her island, would have to drink her tea without milk.

Surely those two dear boys will come, she thought. They had concerned themselves about her last night when they did not know her; it seemed more likely that they would do so today. She so convinced herself of this that, in the middle of sipping her tea, she went into the bathroom to make something of her face.

But they did not come and the day went slowly. She watched from the window and it was a dull, watery world she saw. The crisis was over and the seabirds beginning to fly away. She finished writing her letter and propped it up against the clock, which had stopped.

When it was dark she pinned the curtains together again and sat down at the table, simply staring in front of her; at the back of her mind, listening. In the warm living-room of her sister's house, the children in dressing-gowns would be eating their supper by the fire; Roy, home from a football match, would be lying back in his chair. Their faces would be turned intently to the blue-white shifting screen of the television.

Rose's was another world, candlelit, silent, lifeless. The church clock chimed seven and she got up and wound up her own clock and set it right; then sat down again, stiffly, with her hands laid palm downwards on the table like an old woman.

They asked me for fun, she told herself. It was just a boyish lark—quite understandable; a joke they wouldn't dream of repeating. If I ever see them again, other week-ends, they'll nod, maybe, and smile; that's all; not that, if their mother's with them. At their age, they never look back or do the same thing twice.

As she had come towards middle-age, she had developed a sentimental fondness for young men—especially those she called the undergraduate type, spoilt, reckless, gay, with long scarves twisted round their necks. Roger had, as he predicted, brought out the maternal in her. Humbly, with great enjoyment, she had listened to their banter, the family jokes, a language hardly understood by her, whom they had briskly teased but gallantly drawn in. So the hours must have passed.

Their mother won't be best pleased about the carpet, she thought, and she got up and took the last cigarette from the packet.

All of Sunday the water receded. Morning and evening the church bells rang across the meadows in which ridges and hillocks of sodden grass stood up. One or two cars splashed down the lane during the afternoon, keeping to the crown of the road and making a great wash.

By Monday morning the garden path was high and nearly dry. Rose looked over the banisters at the wet, muddy entrance and found it difficult to believe that the swan had ever swum about down there. It was over.

She could go out now and post her letter and fetch what she wanted from the shops; and on Friday Gilbert would come, and on all the Fridays' after, she supposed, though she could never be quite sure. So she would survive from year to year, and one day soon would begin a diet and perhaps save some money for her old age.

It was like being in prison, she thought of the last few days. Sunday had been endless and she had cried a little and gone to bed early, but remained awake, yet on other Sundays she most often stayed indoors all day or pottered about the garden, and had always been contented.

Now she was free and she put on her coat, took the letter from the shelf, and looked out of the window once more to make sure that it was really safe to go out and walk on the earth again. And that really was the sum of her freedom—for the first time the truth of it dawned on her. She could go out and walk to the shops, like a prisoner on parole, and spend the money Gilbert had given her, or save it if she could, and then she would turn back and return, for there was nothing else to do.

The clock ticked—a sound she knew too well. There were other sounds which were driven into her existence—the church bells and the milkman's rattle—and they no longer sufficed and had begun to torment her. Her contentment with them had come to an end.

The exciting thought occurred to her that it was in her power to fly away from them for ever. Nothing could stop her.

For a moment she stood quite still, her head tilted as if she were listening, and then she suddenly turned her handbag upside down and tipped the money on the table. "What will Gilbert do?" she wondered, as she counted the coins. He would never have visualised her doing anything impulsive, would stand in the porch bewildered, amazed that she did not open the door at once and, when he had sorted out his own key and let himself in, his face would be a picture, she thought.

"I'd like to see it," she said aloud, and scooped up the money and dropped it back into her bag. Where would he break his journey that night? she wondered. Or would he perhaps go petulantly home to his wife?

She was smiling as she quickly packed her suitcase, almost shook with laughter when she slammed the door and set off down the muddy path. Such a dreadful mess she had left behind her.

She felt warm in her fur coat as she picked her way down the lane. The floods had shifted the gravel about and made deep ruts, the hedgerows were laced with scum; but the valley was recovering, cows were being driven back to the pastures and hundreds of birds were out scavenging.

The letter was still in Rose's hand but, as she stopped for a moment by a stile to rest, she suddenly screwed it up and tossed it over the hedge, knowing she would reach Beryl first.

THE SMILE OF WINTER

Angela Carter

Because there are no seagulls here, the only sound is the resonance of the sea. This coastal region is quite flat, so that an excess of sky bears down with an intolerable weight, pressing the essence out of everything beneath it for it imposes such a burden on us that we have all been forced inward on ourselves in an introspective sombreness intensified by the perpetual abrasive clamour of the sea. When the sun goes down it is very cold and then I easily start crying because the winter moon pierces my heart. The winter moon is surrounded by an extraordinary darkness, the logical antithesis of the supernal clarity of the day; in this darkness, the dogs in every household howl together at the sight of a star, as if the stars were unnatural things. But, from morning until evening, a hallucinatory light floods the shore and a cool, glittering sun transfigures everything so brilliantly that the beach looks like a desert and the ocean like a mirage.

But the beach is never deserted. Far from it. At times, there is even a silent crowd of people—women who come in groups to turn the fish they have laid out to dry on bamboo racks; Sunday trippers; solitary anglers, even. Sometimes trucks drive up and down the beach to and fro from the next headland and after school is over children come to improvise games of baseball with sticks and a dead crab delivered to them by the tide. The children wear peaked, yellow caps; their heads are perfectly round. Their faces are perfectly bland, the colour as well as the shape of brown eggs. They giggle when they see me because I am white and pink while they themselves are such a serviceable, unanimous beige. Besides all these visitors, the motorcyclists who come at night have left deep grooves behind them in the sand as if to say: "I have been here."

When the shadows of the evening lie so thickly on the beach it looks as though nobody as dusted it for years, the motorcyclists come out. That is their favourite time. They have marked out a course among the dunes with red wooden pegs and ride round it at amazing speeds. They come when they please. Sometimes they come in the early morning but, most often, by owl-light. They announce their presence with a fanfare of opened throttles. They grow their hair long and it flies out behind them like black flags, motorcyclists as beautiful as the outriders of death in the film *Orphée*. I wish they were not so beautiful; if they were not so beautiful and so inaccessible to me, then I should feel less lonely, although, after all, I came here in order to be lonely.

The beach is full of the garbage of the ocean. The waves leave torn, translucent furls of polythene wrappings too tough for even this sea's iron stomach; chipped jugs that once held rice wine; single sea-boots freighted with sand; broken beer bottles and, once, a brown dog stiff and dead washed up as far as the pine trees which, subtly warped by the weather, squat on their hunkers at the end of my garden, where the dry soil transforms itself to sand.

Already the pines are budding this year's cones. Each blunt, shaggy bough is tipped with a small, lightly furred growth just like the prick of a little puppy while the dry, brown cones of last year still cling to the rough stems though now these are so insecure a touch will bring them bounding down. But, all in all, the pines have a certain intransigence. They dig their roots into dry soil full of seashells and strain backwards in the wind that blows directly from Alaska. They are absolutely exposed to the weather and yet as indifferent as the weather. The indifference of this Decembral littoral suits my forlorn mood for I am a sad woman by nature, no doubt about that; how unhappy I should be in a happy world! This country has the most rigorous romanticism in the world and they think a woman who lives by herself should accentuate her melancholy with surroundings of sentimental dilapidation. I have read about all the abandoned lovers in their old books eating their hearts out like Mariana in so many moated granges; their gardens are overgrown with goosegrass and mugwort, their mud walls are falling to pieces and their carp pools scaled over with water-lily pads. Everything combines with the forlorn mood of the châtelaine to procure a moving image of poignant desolation. In this country you do not need to think, but only to look, and soon you think you understand everything.

The old houses in the village are each one dedicated to seclusion and court an individual sequestered sadness behind the weather-stained, unpainted wooden shutters they usually keep closed. It is a gloomy, aridly aesthetic architecture based on the principle of perpetual regression. The houses are heavily shingled and the roofs are the shapes and colours of waves frozen on a grey day. In the mornings, they dismantle the outer screens to let fresh air blow through and, as you walk past, you can see that all the inner walls are also sliding screens, though this time of stiff paper, and you can glimpse endlessly receding perspectives of interiors in brownish tones, as if everything had been heavily varnished some time ago; and, though these perspectives can be altered at will, the fresh rooms they make when they shift the screens about always look exactly the same as the old rooms. And all the matted interiors are the same, anyway.

Through the gaping palings of certain fences, I sometimes see a garden so harmoniously in tune with the time of year it looks forsaken. But sometimes all these fragile habitations of unpainted wood; and the still lives, or *natures mortes*, of rusting water pumps and withered chrysanthemums in backyards; and the discarded fishing boats pulled up on the sand and left to rot away—sometimes the whole village looks forsaken. This is, after all, the season of abandonment, of the suspension of vitality, a long cessation of vigour in which we must cultivate our stoicism. Everything has put on the desolate smile of winter. Outside my shabby front door, I have a canal, like Mariana in a moated grange; beyond the skulking pines at the back, there is only the ocean. The winter moon pierces my heart. I weep.

But when I went out on the beach this morning with the skin on my face starched with dried tears so I could feel my cheeks crackle in the wind, I found the sea had washed me up a nice present—two pieces of driftwood. One was a forked chunk like a pair of wooden trousers and the other was a larger, greyish, frayed root the shape of the paw of a ragged lion. I collect driftwood and set it up among the pine trees in picturesque attitudes on the edge of the beach and then I strike a picturesque attitude myself beside them as I watch the constantly agitated waves, for here we all strike picturesque attitudes and that is why we are so beautiful. Sometimes I imagine that one night the riders will stop at the end of my garden and I will hear the heels of their boots crunch on the friable carpet of last year's shed cones and then there will be a hesitant rattle of knuckles on the seaward-facing door and they will wait in ceremonious silence until I come, for their bodies are only images.

My pockets always contain a rasping sediment of sand because I fill them with shells when I go onto the beach. The vast majority of these shells are round, sculptural forms the colour of a brown egg, with warm, creamy insides. They have a classical simplicity. The scarcely perceptible indentations of their surfaces flow together to produce a texture as subtly matt as that of a petal which is as satisfying to touch as Japanese skin. But there are also pure white shells heavily ridged on the outside but within of a marmoreal smoothness and these come in hinged pairs.

There is still a third kind of shell, though I find these less often. They are curlicued, shaped like turbans and dappled with pink, of a substance so thin the ocean easily grinds away the outer husk to lay bare their spiralline cores. They are often decorated with baroque, infinitesimal swags of calcified parasites. They are the smallest of all the shells but by far the most intricate. When I picked up one of those shells, I found it contained the bright pink, dried, detached limb of a tiny sea creature like a dehydrated memory. Sometimes a litter of dropped fish lies among the shells. Each fish reflects the sky with the absolute purity of a Taoist mirror.

The fish have fallen off the racks on which they have been put out to dry. These bamboo racks spread with fish stand on trestles all along the beach as if a feast was laid for the entire prefecture but nobody had come to eat it. Close to the village, there are whole paddocks filled with bamboo racks. In one of these paddocks, a tethered goat crops grass. The fish are as shiny as fish of tin and the size of my little finger. Once dried, they are packed in plastic bags and sold to flavour soup.

The women lay them out. They come every day to turn them and, when the fish are ready, they pile up the racks and carry them to the packing sheds. There are great numbers of these raucously silent, and well-muscled, intimidating women.

The cruel wind burns port-wine whorls on their dour, inexpressive faces. All wear dark or drab-coloured trousers pinched in at the ankle and either short rubber boots or split-toed socks on their feet. A layer of jacket sweaters and a loose, padded, cotton jacket gives them a squat, top-heavy look, as if they would not fall over, only rock malevolently to and fro if you pushed them. Over their jackets, they wear short, immaculate aprons trimmed with coarse lace and they tie white baboushkas round their heads or sometimes wind a kind of wimple over the ears and round the throat. They are truculent and aggressive. They stare at me with open curiosity tinged with hostility. When they laugh, they display treasuries of gold teeth and their hands are as hard as those of eighteenth-century prize-fighters, who also used to pickle their fists in brine. They make me feel that either I or they are deficient in femininity and I suppose it must be I since most of them hump about an organic lump of baby on their backs, inside their coats. It seems that only women people the village because most of the men are out on the sea. Early in the morning, I go out to watch the winking and blinking of the fishing boats on the water, which, just before dawn, has turned a deep violet.

The moist and misty mornings after a storm obscure the horizon for then the ocean has turned into the sky and the wind and waves have realigned the contours of the dunes. The wet sand is as dark and more yieldingly solid than fudge and walking across a panful is a promenade in the Kingdom of Sweets. The waves leave behind them glinting striations of salt and forcibly mould the foreshore into the curvilinear abstractions of cliffs, bays, inlets, curvilinear tumuli like sculpture of Arp. But the storms themselves are a raucous music and turn my house into an Aeolian xylophone. All night long, the wind bangs and rattles away at every wooden surface; the house is a sounding box and even on the quietest nights the paper windows let through the wind that rattles softly in the pines.

Sometimes the lights of the midnight riders scrawl brilliant hieroglyphs across the panes, especially on moonless nights, when I am alone in a landscape of extraordinary darkness, and I am a little frightened when I see their headlamps and hear their rasping engines for then they see the spawn of the negated light and to have driven straight out of the sea, which is just as mysterious as the night, even, and also its perfect image, for the sea is an inversion of the known and occupies half, or more, of the world, just as night does; whilst different peoples also live in the countries of the night.

They all wear leather jackets bristling with buckles, and high-heeled boots. They cannot buy such gaudy apparel in the village because the village shops only sell useful things such as paraffin, quilts and things to eat. And all the colours in the village are subfusc and equivocal, those of wood tinted bleakly by the weather and of lifeless wintry vegetation. When I sometimes see an orange tree hung with gold balls like a magic trick, it does nothing but stress by contrast the prevailing static sobriety of everything, which combines to smile in chorus the desolate smile of winter. On rainy nights when there is a winter moon bright enough to pierce the heart, I often wake to find my face still wet with tears so that I know I have been crying.

When the sun is low in the west, the beams become individually visible and fall with a peculiar, lateral intensity across the beach, flushing out long shadows from the grains of sand and these beams seem to penetrate to the very hearts of the incoming waves which look, then, as if they were lit from within. Before they topple forward, they bulge outward in the swollen shapes and artfully flawed incandescence of Art Nouveau glass, as if the translucent bodies of the images they contain within them were trying to erupt, for the bodies of the creatures of the sea are images, I am convinced of that. At this time of day, the sea turns amazing colours—the brilliant, chemical green of the sea in nineteenth-century tinted postcards; or a blue far too cerulean for early evening; or sometimes it shines with such metallic brilliance I can hardly hear to look at it. Smiling my habitual winter smile, I stand at the end of my garden attended by a pack of green bears while I watch the constantly agitated white lace cuffs on the colourful sleeves of the Pacific.

Different peoples inhabit countries of the ocean and some of their emanations undulate past me when I walk along the beach to the village on one of those rare, bleak, sullen days, spectral wraiths of sand blowing to various inscrutable meeting places on blind currents of the Alaskan wind. They twine around my ankles in serpentine caresses and they have eyes of sand but some of the other creatures have eyes of solid water and when the women move among trays of fish I think they, too, are sea creatures, spiny, ocean-bottom-growing flora and if a tidal wave consumed the village—as it could do tomorrow, for there are no hills or sea walls to protect us—there, under the surface, life would go on just as before, the sea goat still nibbling, the shops still doing a roaring trade in octopus and pickled turnips greens, the women going about their silent business because everything is as silent as if it were under the water, anyway, and the very air is as heavy as water and warps the light so that one sees as if one's eyes were made of water.

Do not think I do not realise what I am doing. I am making a composition using the following elements: the winter beach; the winter moon; the ocean; the women; the pine trees; the riders; the driftwood; the shells; the shapes of darkness and the shapes of water; and the refuse. These are all inimical to my loneliness because of their indifference to it. Out of these pieces of inimical indifference, I intend to represent the desolate smile of winter which, as you must have gathered, is the smile I wear.

COPYRIGHT NOTICES

'The Prisoner' by Elizabeth Berridge reproduced with permission of David Higham Associates on behalf of the Estate of Elizabeth Berridge.

'The Cut Finger' by Frances Bellerby reproduced with permission of David Higham Associates on behalf of the Estate of Frances Bellerby.

'The Thames Spread Out' by Elizabeth Taylor reproduced with permission of Johnson & Alcock Ltd on behalf of the Estate of Elizabeth Taylor.

'The Smile of Winter' from *Fireworks: Nine Profane Pieces* by Angela Carter. Published by Quartet, 1974. Copyright © The Estate of Angela Carter. Reproduced by permission of the Estate c/o Rogers, Coleridge & White Ltd., 20 Powis Mews, London W11 1JN.

Introduction to Sally Elizabeth von Arnim

One Year's Time Angela Milne

Sing Me Who You Are Elizabeth Berridge

The Home Penelope Mortimer

STORIES FOR CHRISTMAS and the festive season

War Among Ladies Eleanor Scott

STRANGE JOURNEY MAUD CAIRNES

KEEPING UP APPEARANCES ROSE MACAULAY

A PIN TO SEE THE PEEPSHOW F. TENNYSON JESSE

THE LOVE CHILD EDITH OLIVIER

WHICH WAY? THEODORA BENSON

Sally on the Rocks Winifred Boggs

Tension E. M. Delafield

Mamma Diana Tutton

O, The Brave Music Dorothy Evelyn Smith

Tea Is So Intoxicating Mary Essex

FATHER ELIZABETH VON ARNIM

DANGEROUS AGES ROSE MACAULAY

CHATTERTON SQUARE E. H. YOUNG

My Husband Simon Mollie Panter-Downes

The Tree of Heaven May Sinclair

OTHER TITLES IN THE WOMEN WRITERS SERIES

The Tree of Heaven by May Sinclair
My Husband Simon by Mollie Panter-Downes
Chatterton Square by E. H. Young
Dangerous Ages by Rose Macaulay
Father by Elizabeth von Arnim
O, The Brave Music by Dorothy Evelyn Smith
Tea Is So Intoxicating by Mary Essex
Tension by E. M. Delafield
Sally on the Rocks by Winifred Boggs
Which Way? by Theodora Benson
A Pin to See the Peepshow by F. Tennyson Jesse
The Love Child by Edith Olivier
Keeping Up Appearances by Rose Macaulay
Strange Journey by Maud Cairnes
War Among Ladies by Eleanor Scott
Stories for Christmas and the Festive Season (an anthology)
The Home by Penelope Mortimer
Sing Me Who You Are by Elizabeth Berridge
One Year's Time by Angela Milne
Introduction to Sally by Elizabeth von Arnim

ALSO AVAILABLE

In the night the snow came.
She awoke on Christmas morning in that unmistakable light, coming up from the earth and shining between her curtains.

Celebrate Christmas through the creative minds of a host of authors, including Beryl Bainbridge, Maeve Binchy, Richmal Crompton, Alice Munro and Elizabeth von Arnim. From the delightful consequences of decorating the tree by Stella Gibbons to a disorientating encounter at 35,000 feet on a Christmas Day flight by Muriel Spark, an amateur pantomime by Stella Margetson and a New Year's resolution by Alice Childress, these stories are sure to fortify you over the Christmas period.